"Can you  *this?"*

Jackson aske ... kissing her a ...

"We have to stop. The McLeans are almost my family." Dawn had trouble catching her breath.

"This isn't about them, it's about us—the way you feel, the way I feel, the way it is between us...and has been since that day up on the mountain." Jackson's intensity couldn't be denied.

"You're here to hurt them."

"No, I'm going to claim my own." He spoke in a fierce murmur. "No one will take what is mine from me. Including you."

Dawn gasped in shock. "I'm not a bone to win from your brother."

Jackson's face softened momentarily. "There isn't a match. I've seen you with him. You don't share *this* with anyone but me. Only me."

And God help her, it was true.

Dear Reader,

The blissful days of summer may be drawing to a close, but love is just beginning to unfold for six special couples at Special Edition!

This month's THAT'S MY BABY! title is brought to you by reader-favorite Nikki Benjamin. *The Surprise Baby* is a heartfelt marriage of convenience story featuring an aloof CEO whose rigid rules about intimacy—and fatherhood—take a nosedive when an impulsive night of wedded bliss results in a surprise bundle of joy. You won't want to miss this tale about the wondrous power of love.

Fasten your seat belts! In these reunion romances, a trio of lovelorn ladies embark on the rocky road to true love. *The Wedding Ring Promise,* by bestselling author Susan Mallery, features a feisty heroine embarking on the adventure of a lifetime with the gorgeous rebel from her youth. Next, a willful spitfire succumbs to the charms of the tough-talkin' cowboy from her past in *A Family Kind of Guy* by Lisa Jackson—book one in her new FOREVER FAMILY miniseries. And in *Temporary Daddy,* by Jennifer Mikels, an orphaned baby draws an unlikely couple back together—for good!

Also don't miss *Warrior's Woman* by Laurie Paige—a seductive story about the healing force of a tender touch; and forbidden love was never more enticing than when a pair of star-crossed lovers fulfill their true destiny in *Meant To Be Married* by Ruth Wind.

I hope you enjoy each and every story to come!

Sincerely,

Karen Taylor Richman,
Senior Editor

Please address questions and book requests to:
Silhouette Reader Service
U.S.: 3010 Walden Ave., P.O. Box 1325, Buffalo, NY 14269
Canadian: P.O. Box 609, Fort Erie, Ont. L2A 5X3

LAURIE PAIGE

WARRIOR'S WOMAN

Silhouette®

SPECIAL EDITION®

Published by Silhouette Books

America's Publisher of Contemporary Romance

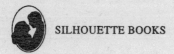

SILHOUETTE BOOKS

ISBN 0-373-24193-3

WARRIOR'S WOMAN

Copyright © 1998 by Olivia M. Hall

LAURIE PAIGE

was recently presented with the *Affaire de Coeur* Readers' Choice Silver Pen Award for Favorite Contemporary Author. In addition, she was a 1994 Romance Writers of America (RITA) finalist for Best Traditional Romance for her book *Sally's Beau*. She reports romance is blooming in her part of northern California. With the birth of her second grandson, she finds herself madly in love with three wonderful males—"all hero material." So far, her husband hasn't complained about the other men in her life.

Chapter One

Dawn Ericson plucked a sprig of sage and rubbed it between her fingers. The aroma pleased her, but the herb wasn't the one she wanted. She walked farther up the mountain, following the path of a tiny creek that was no more than three feet wide at this point.

The plant she sought supposedly grew along rocky creek banks here in the Sierra Nevada of northern California. The medicinal herb was said to be good for "women's woes." Women could certainly use that. Smiling, she continued her exploration.

She stepped across the stream, then paused and listened intently, puzzled. The sound she heard was most definitely a chant.

The low, melodious voice was masculine. Barely audible, it tantalized and piqued her curiosity, luring her higher up the mountainside and deeper into the woods.

She moved toward the sound, her footsteps disguised by the running water, her curiosity increasing as she drew closer to the source. Pausing in the shadows at the edge of a clearing, she stared in wonder at the woodland scene.

A man hunkered beside a wood fire on a sandy strand beside the creek. The muscular breadth of his chest, the firm flex of his back and shoulders, the sinewy length of his legs—all were masculine and powerful.

He wore a pair of faded cutoffs and jogging shoes.

Hair as black as a raven's wing flowed to his shoulders. His hands, long-fingered and strong looking, worked skillfully as he secured a rabbit on a peeled willow stick and propped it over the fire.

Enchanted, she remained silent and watched, admiring his ease here in the woodland setting.

When he turned aside after finishing his task, his face came into view in sharp profile. A bolt of lightning hit her nerves, spreading out to every part of her body, making her heart pound. Something akin to fear swept over her.

She knew who he was.

Not that she'd ever met the intruder, but she'd seen a newspaper photo. From the article, she knew a lot about him and his life. For the past three months he had been the subject of gossip and speculation in these parts.

Every sense urged her to flee, to tell others of his presence and warn them. But alert them to what? That the unwanted and hated heir was on the ranch? That the bastard son had arrived at last?

Transfixed by the primordial scene, she didn't move, although she knew, with a certainty beyond any doubt, that this sleek, powerful creature, as beautiful as he was, was there to wreak havoc on the McLean family.

And on her?

The question slipped unbidden into her mind. She felt the flow of strife and contention all around her. It didn't take a psychic to know he was going to disrupt their lives. He would hurt those she loved, and there wasn't a thing she could do to prevent it.

Instead of slipping away so she could warn her friends she stood still while he finished his song. An irresistible impulse, as instinctive as the flight of a bird, compelled her to take the step that would disclose her presence and confront him.

But as she walked from the shadows into the warm June sunlight, another feeling—that he'd been expecting her, that he was preparing the meal for *them*—swept over her. The whole scene was surreal, with a sense of timelessness about it. As if it were meant to be…

She frowned, confused by the conflicting thoughts that darted through her mind.

At that moment, he glanced her way, a Swiss Army knife in his hand. No flash of surprise showed in his face. His gaze took her in as thoroughly as a warrior sizing up the enemy. He'd known she was there.

She hesitated, not sure what he might do next, before stepping into the clearing. She kept her distance.

Sensing an aura of fury coupled with a fierce pride, she didn't want to be close enough to be grabbed in a sudden lunge.

He stood and turned with a smooth ripple of muscle, and she realized her caution was useless. He could have been upon her in a second if he'd wished.

Transfixed, she took in his primitive but powerful appearance. His naturally dusky skin was tanned to a rich bronze and glowed with health in the dappled light of the sun shining through the trees.

His eyes were green. Like his father's. Like his brother's. The embedded golden flecks caught a stray beam of sunlight and flashed like molten gold as he stared at her, tension in every line of his body.

"Jackson," she said, testing the sound of the name.

He didn't speak, but his face hardened with a subtle shifting of muscle tension.

"You are Jackson McLean, aren't you?"

"Firebird," he corrected, hatred flashing like fox fire in his eyes. "Jackson Firebird is my name."

In the swift, harsh words, she heard the fierce denial of the father who hadn't claimed his son while he'd been alive. The son refused to take the father's name now that the man was dead and had willed half the ranch and his holdings to his illegitimate son.

She thought of the other son and the grieving widow. There was anger and grief yet to be worked through. And more to come. What a tangled web John Jackson McLean had left behind for his sons to unravel. A premonition that she would be in the midst of the unraveling hit her.

* * *

Jackson watched the woman with a wariness honed into him by years of experience. She was one of the loveliest creatures he'd ever seen…and as forbidden to his touch as the priceless works of art in a museum his mother had once taken him to.

The museum guard had yelled at him as he'd reached toward a porcelain figurine that had fascinated him. The woman before him fascinated him as much as that dainty statue had when he was ten. He'd been watching her for days.

Her white-blond hair lay smooth and straight over her shoulders. Her eyes were light blue, as luminous as moonstone. She was about five-eight, he estimated. At six feet plus, he was taller, but he didn't tower over her.

Her legs were outlined in the faded jeans she wore. Her breasts thrust against a T-shirt. A jacket was tied by the sleeves around her waist. A fanny pack rode low on her slender but feminine hips.

She was as fine-boned as a Thoroughbred. Her face, like her body, was long and slender but put together in pleasing proportions so that the overall effect was one of refined loveliness. Her skin was milk fair and looked as soft as velvet, as smooth as satin.

She was a woman so far beyond his expectations, he would never have dreamed her into existence even in his wildest imaginings. Anger, hot and useless, welled in him. He ground it into dust by force of will.

''There's enough for two,'' he said, indicating the rabbit on the spit. His voice was husky, with undertones of sexual interest. His body stirred.

She blinked those incredible eyes once, the wariness in their azure depths increasing. She should be apprehensive; he wanted her with an intensity that was unnerving.

He wanted to hear her voice again. It was soft, but not breathless or weak. The tone had depth. She was an alto rather than a soprano. He liked that.

"You own a ranch down the road from the McLean spread. You live in a house there with an older woman," he said when she didn't speak, which he took as a rejection of his offer.

The refusal to share the simple meal didn't surprise him. She was on the other side—the one that included his enemies—his father's widow, Margaret McLean, and their son, Hunter McLean. The legitimate son.

"My mother," she affirmed. "She raises herbs for health-food stores and I help her out."

"And you board and train horses for pleasure riding, ranch work or the Western-show circuit for rich dudes who haven't any idea how to do it themselves."

He'd reconnoitered the area for ten days, watching the comings and goings of all those at the McLean ranch. This woman and her mother lived down the road and visited almost daily. It had been easy to include them in his observations. And easy to find out from local gossip that they were lifelong friends of the McLeans. More than friends; rumor had it that McLean and this woman were engaged.

"The land belongs to us equally. We're partners." A smile bloomed over lips the color of roses.

His heart gave a lurch, then thudded like a captured antelope's. He frowned, shocked at his body's betrayal of desire for this woman who was friend to his enemies.

The smile disappeared. "You'd better tend to your lunch." She gestured to the spit. "It smells delicious."

She wasn't one of those women put off by meat that didn't come shrink-wrapped in plastic. He wasn't sure if this surprised him or merely fueled his anger that she was so near perfection and could never be his.

Or maybe she could. Briefly. Lots of white women liked the idea of a Native American for a lover. A half-breed was the same thing in their eyes.

"Are you going to join me?" he asked bluntly, sounding as friendly as an irritated porcupine.

She considered, then nodded. "I brought some food," she murmured in a voice like thick honey. "Carrots. Snow peas. A pumpernickel roll. An apple and a tangerine. Two pieces of string cheese."

Her hands were graceful as she removed the food from the fanny pack, which had a picture of Minnie Mouse on it. No rings of any kind adorned her fingers.

She placed the items on a flat rock he'd found and moved closer to the fire; then she chose another stone to perch on. "This is one of my favorite places. It's private here, but if you climb those rocks, you can see Honey Lake and the valley around it." She gestured toward the ridge of granite that rose above their heads.

She reminded him of a white dove. He wondered if she would take food from his hand if he offered it. Odd, but he wanted to feed her. Tension gripped his chest as a vision of them eating together, of her laughing and flirting with him, inviting his touch, came to him.

He shook his head slightly to clear the fantasy. He'd learned early on not to dream of the impossible.

Once, he'd hoped his father would appear and bring him home to this big, fine ranch and claim him as a son the way he did the other one. It hadn't happened. And never would, now that the old man had kicked up his heels for the last time this past March.

"When will lunch be ready?" the woman asked.

"Another half hour. I was going to bathe," he added roughly, the anger at her resurfacing for unknowingly having destroyed the peace he'd found in this place.

"Go ahead. I'll turn the spit." She peered up at him with a wry smile. "My father taught me how to cook over an open fire. I won't let it burn."

Mid-twenties, he decided, studying her face. She was too self-assured to be younger, even though her face was as smooth as an unmarked sheet of rose-toned parchment paper.

Not too young for his twenty-eight years, although he felt much older. Bastards matured faster than those raised in the bosom of the legitimate family. He shrugged the thought aside. "It wouldn't be the first time I've had to eat burned meat."

"Well, you won't today. Go on." She waved him away.

He walked to the other side of a rock outcropping and removed soap and clean clothes from his saddlebags. A black stallion grazed nearby. The horse swiveled an ear toward him, but continued eating.

The animal hadn't given a warning of the woman's presence earlier, even though the wind was from her direction. Odd, that. Obviously the stallion hadn't been alarmed by her approach. Maybe it wasn't so odd. She seemed as much a part of the woodland scene as a sylph.

Jackson shook his head again, trying to dislodge the fantasy that had formed in his mind—that nature intended the woman to be his, a gift for surviving...for persevering...for coming to this place although every instinct urged him to cut and run before it was too late.

"Coyote laughs," his grandfather would have said.

He searched silently in a semicircle around the camp, finding nothing but her trail along the stream. She'd come alone and on foot. To see him? No, she couldn't have known he was here. He'd been careful not to be seen. Although, he admitted, she had almost taken him by surprise today.

She usually worked with her horses and the plants from dawn until dark. Her other excursions were to the small town out on Highway 395 where it wound close to Honey Lake here in the mountains of northern California. He circled back the way he'd come, satisfied she'd come alone and not as some kind of ruse to distract him from a surprise attack.

The cold water made him gasp and clench his teeth when he finally stepped into the creek a few yards above the camp where the woman watched over their noon meal. He waded into a pool he'd found the week before and began to wash the dust away after a morning spent scouting this section of the ranch, then catching the rabbit for his meal.

He was low on rations, but he wasn't ready to report in at the ranch house. Not yet. Not until he knew the lay of the land like the palm of his hand. He might need a bolt-hole if things got too rough. He'd once had the starch beaten out of him for daring to set foot on the McLean ranch.

Ducking under the icy water that came from snow melting higher in the mountains, he rinsed the soap out of his hair. He wondered what the woman had thought, seeing him with his hair unbound and wearing only cutoffs.

A savage. That was probably how she saw him.

But she hadn't been afraid of him—wary, yes, but not afraid. There had been fire in those cool depths as she confronted him. But the fire wasn't for him. She came from the bosom of his enemies. He'd better remember that.

However, her every gesture had bespoken a gentle femininity, in spite of her clothing. She often wore long skirts and loose blouses, especially in the evenings after her chores were done. Her hands were so graceful in their movements, he could imagine how they would feel caressing a man.

She was a listening woman, this Nordic beauty who smelled of wild sage and was comfortable alone in the woods. She'd stood quietly as he'd recited an ancient prayer of thanks to the rabbit's spirit for giving him sustenance.

A woman of rare understanding.

He would have scalped her if she'd applauded like a tourist at a sideshow. But she hadn't.

With a soft expletive, he cursed aloud. He knew very little about her, other than her name. Dawn Ericson. Dawn. The beginning of light—

A movement—the same that had alerted him to her presence earlier—jerked his gaze to the ring of boulders that nearly surrounded the pool.

"Lunch!" she called.

A woman's knowledge of life was in her eyes as she gazed at him. He was naked but for the water that frothed around his waist. She had known from the first that he'd wanted her. It wasn't something a man could hide. She wanted him, too, but didn't know it yet.

It was troubling, this way of thinking about her.

She stood on the rock for another moment, her eyes locked with his. Golden arcs of awareness bent the space around them until it seemed they were nearer although neither had moved.

He nodded. The cold water had had no effect on his libido. Heat pounded through him, and he wanted her in the pool with him, holding on as he slid into her warmth....

After she jumped off the rock and disappeared behind the trees, he finished quickly and headed for the bank. He wiped a bandanna over the clinging droplets of water, then slipped into jeans, shirt, socks and boots. He hung the freshly washed cutoffs over a branch to dry. After combing his hair, he tied a rawhide thong around it at his nape.

He inhaled deeply, then headed around the out-cropping of granite to rejoin his guest.

Dawn heard his approach and knew he'd deliber-ately made noise in order not to startle her. He carried an armload of branches and dropped them beside the fire pit.

"I think the rabbit is done. It's brown all over," she added unnecessarily.

His appearance in boots and regular clothing added to his height and breadth, making him appear more formidable in civilized garb than in the more casual outfit.

"I'll get the plates," he said. He retrieved two metal plates from a saddlebag and handed one to her. He deftly sectioned the rabbit, then gave half to her and kept the other half for himself.

She divided her food evenly between them. "I'm Dawn Ericson," she told him, picking up a joint of meat.

"Dawn," he repeated.

Her name sounded intimate, sexy, rolling off his tongue. He said it as if mulling the word over, search-ing out every nuance of meaning. He glanced into her eyes, then at his plate. "It suits." He didn't sound happy about it.

"Are you checking out the ranch?"

"Maybe."

"You're due there on June fifth. Friday."

He said nothing.

"That's two days from now, in case you've lost track of time while you've been reconnoitering the place. How long have you been here?"

His gaze narrowed. "A little over a week. Are you going to report me?" he challenged.

"I don't know," she said truthfully. The ranch was half his, so he could come and go as he wished. She understood why he might want to look around first. He wasn't exactly a welcome guest. "I can tell you who lives on the ranch and who your neighbors are, if you'd like."

"I know who lives on the ranch. Hunter McLean. There's a three-year-old son, but no wife. The woman in the wheelchair is his mother. She has a companion who spends her days in the main house but lives in another one with an older man and a younger one."

Dawn nodded. "Hunter's wife was my sister. A cattle truck overturned, killing her and my father. Margaret McLean, his mother, was injured in a different auto accident years ago. Anna and Russell Hamilton are the couple. Anna keeps house for Margaret and cooks for the ranch. Russell is the ranch foreman. Their son works on the ranch, too, along with four other hands."

"There are twenty more on the logging operations."

"That's separate. The company that harvests the trees provides the logging crew."

"They're clear-cutting over near Hot Springs Peak."

She was surprised. "You're sure? Hunter will be angry to hear that. It isn't part of the deal."

"Huh," he said skeptically, sounding very much like his half brother.

"Everyone is talking about the will. Until his death, no one knew John McLean had another son."

"Hunter McLean and his mother knew."

She didn't think so, but she didn't argue. "Hunter is bitter that his father left you half of the ranch. He's always considered it his domain. His roots go deep here."

No emotion showed in the bronze face or the green eyes so like Hunter's. "Sometimes a man has to give up his dream and face reality. I'm half owner of the JMc ranch now."

"Yes. John's will is airtight, according to his attorney. Your attorney thinks so, too."

"I'm sure his wife and son have looked into every law on the books in order to break it." Jackson hadn't been able to make up his mind about the ranch and whether he wanted to appear there or not. His father had requested that he live part of each year for five years at the homestead. It wasn't a condition for getting the inheritance, only a request.

Until this moment, he hadn't decided whether he'd go there or not on Friday. His attorney thought he should, to stake his claim, so to speak. Jackson hadn't attended the funeral or the reading of the will.

"Do you intend to live there for a while?"

"Yes," he said, making the decision at this moment. "Any reason why I shouldn't?"

"None. It'll be hard, though. Hunter is furious. His mother is beside herself. She hates you."

She stated the facts without trying to pretty them up. He liked that in her, even as he snorted in contempt. Hatred was nothing new in his life. He could handle it.

"She sees another woman's son usurping her son's place. It's only to be expected. It must hurt very much, knowing your husband fathered another son by another woman."

He rejected the pity in her eyes. "Don't expect any kindness from me," he stated, remembering his past reception at the ranch house.

Dawn tore a bite from the pumpernickel. Chewing on it and a carrot stick, she thought over the situation that would occur when Jackson appeared at the ranch. He was so different from Hunter, who was fair-skinned and brawny compared to this man's sinewy length. But both men had dark hair. And those green eyes with the gold flecks were the same—another legacy from John Jackson McLean.

The fact that Jackson had his father's name had made Margaret McLean that much angrier when she'd found a copy of her husband's will before the reading and learned of the split inheritance. She'd destroyed the copy, but it hadn't mattered. The attorney had the original.

Dawn sensed the dark clouds of the gathering storm looming beyond the horizon. She thought of the Four Horsemen of the Apocalypse, galloping wildly toward them with their evil wares.

The road ahead would be laden with trouble. "No two ways about it," Russ, the foreman, would have said. Another tremor of premonition ran through her.

She studied Jackson, this harsh outsider who was the renegade son of the rancher's indiscretion with another woman. There would be deep hurt and anger before this storm played itself out. He would be a daily reminder of that betrayal if he stayed.

"There's no need for you to stay here," she said, thinking of Hunter and Margaret. "It wasn't part of the will. According to Hunter," she added, "his father—your father—only made a request."

She heard the rejection in her own words. *Outsider.* It was what the local people were already calling him. No one had thought he would dare show up. Even the attorney had admitted he'd advised John McLean to leave the young man money if he felt he had to, but not part of the ranch and other operations. She knew Jackson wasn't to blame for his existence, but his presence would be a thorn—

"I don't need your pity."

The harshly spoken words jerked her out of the troubled contemplation of their tangled futures. "I didn't know I'd offered any." She returned his cold glare.

She sensed things she didn't want to admit. It was too late to change the fate that awaited them all. John McLean had seen to that. But…

"Life is going to be hard," she murmured. "For everyone."

"Including you?" He looked skeptical.

"Yes. My mother, too." She shook her head. "She and Hunter's mother have been best friends since their schooldays. I grew up as much in their home as my own."

"You've always lived near the ranch?"

"I was born here. My father tried to raise cattle,

but our holdings are too small for a profitable operation. Mom liked growing herbs. We decided to try it commercially.''

''Why?''

''One of her best friends had a Paiute grandmother. She used to tell us stories of her youth and about gathering herbs for healing and for cooking. We found it fascinating.''

He made a low sound. The corners of his mouth crimped as if in anger. She gazed at his lips, which were thin, but evenly balanced. Their outline was marred by a faint scar running across the upper lip. His teeth were brilliantly white against the bronze skin—when he bothered to smile. His nose was lean and hawkish. His eyes, fringed with black lashes, were beautiful.

A handsome face, full of power and determination. Stubborn, too.

''Medicine woman,'' he muttered, his eyes narrowing as if disliking the idea. ''A medicine woman.''

He shook his head as if the words made him angry. He clenched one hand into a fist. She fully expected him to shake it at the heavens. Instead he spread his fingers, then picked up a piece of meat and ate hungrily.

''Well, not really. Mom and I study herbs, especially the healing ones. I think they can be more effective in our lives than prescription drugs sometimes. But we would never suggest their use for illness without a doctor's advice.''

''Of course,'' he agreed smoothly.

Silence fell between them as they finished eating.

She wondered what Friday would bring when Jackson showed up at the ranch. Ha. That was an easy one. Trouble. Heartache. Resentment. Perhaps violence.

Anyone could see the troubled future concerning this man and his father's determination to make up for the past with an inheritance shared equally between his two sons.

After the meal, Jackson took the plates and washed them in a cup of warm water and put them away. He filled the cup and set it on the coals again, then sat silently contemplating the flames while the water heated. When it was hot, he tossed some dried leaves into the cup, added a dollop of honey from a plastic bottle and handed it to her. The herbal tea turned the hot water reddish brown.

"My grandmother's recipe," he said.

She took a sip. It had a delightful tang. "Rose hips, chamomile, lemon basil. Um, hibiscus. What else?" She took another drink and handed the cup back.

"A secret. Maybe I'll tell you someday." His eyes held a mysterious gleam, as dark and dangerous and enticing as a derelict castle.

"I think you have a lot of secrets, Jackson Firebird McLean," she murmured.

"Maybe." He gazed at her steadily until the intensity became too great.

She looked away and studied the severe peaks of the Sierra Nevada all around them. A breeze caressed her face and stirred her hair. It penetrated her clothing and cooled her suddenly hot skin.

Resentment flared briefly as she was reminded of the fierce winds of discord blowing toward those she loved. Troubled, she studied the man who calmly ate and watched her with an unrelenting gaze.

"What are you going to do here?" she asked, the question erupting unbidden from some deep inner part of her that heaved and swelled like a stormy sea.

"Claim my inheritance," he said in a tone of deadly determination.

"And damn the consequences."

"Yes."

She stood abruptly. "I have to go."

He rose, too, his eyes never leaving hers. "Are you going to tell them I'm here?"

"Yes." She hesitated. It was his ranch and his business, not hers. "Unless you would rather I didn't."

"I would."

Nodding, she turned and headed down the trail, feeling that she'd made a pact with the devil and wondering what she would have to pay for doing it.

Her soul? Would he demand that much of her?

A shiver washed over her. She sped down the mountain as fast as she dared, away from danger...and from fantasy.

Chapter Two

Jackson filled out the registration form for the waiting clerk, hesitated, then added "McLean." There. That should spread the news he was in the area. He smiled grimly and handed the slip to the girl.

She looked at the name. Her jaw dropped in an audible gasp before she caught herself. Her gaze flew to his, then she blushed a torrid pink. "Your room is 204, at the top of the stairs, Mr., uh, Mr. McLean."

Her fingers actually trembled when she handed over the key. He was tempted to do something outrageous, such as say "Boo!" to her.

But he wasn't there to stir up more speculation about himself than already existed. He wanted to clean up, get a good night's sleep and have a hot meal before he faced the McLeans tomorrow. He picked up the duffel bag he'd carried since his youth when he'd been packed off to Indian boarding school at the orders of the white men in charge of Native American affairs and headed for the door. At the time he'd resented being sent away from the ranch and the reservation he'd loved in order to learn the white man's ways.

Glancing back, he saw the girl watching him. Like Dawn Ericson, she had the fair skin of a Nordic blonde, although her hair was darker than Dawn's.

His thoughts lingered on the beautiful intruder who had filled his thoughts yesterday afternoon and his dreams last night while he climbed the stairs and entered his room. He'd known there was going to be trouble when he came to the ranch, but he hadn't expected it to be in the form of a tall, slender woman with hair like silver and eyes like the sky.

Inside, he dropped the duffel on the king-size bed, his imagination immediately springing into overtime as he thought of being there with her. He'd had the same visions last night when he'd snuggled down in his sleeping bag to watch the stars before dropping off. It had been a long time before he'd relaxed enough to sleep.

It would probably be the same tonight.

Grimacing, he stripped and showered, then caught the evening news. After that, he removed the legal papers from the duffel and read them over—just in case he'd missed something. He wanted to be sure of his position before he entered the lion's den tomorrow.

Friday. McLean's mother had hosted a bridge party last Friday afternoon. Dawn's mother had attended.

The daughter had gone up after working with her horses and had dinner with the family. McLean had grilled steaks on the back patio.

The scene had been quite neighborly. Dawn had stayed with McLean while the steaks cooked. They had kissed.

Anger hit him at the memory. Last week, watching them, he'd been merely curious about the woman, wondering if she would be the next Mrs. McLean to join the older woman in the stone-and-timber ranch house. Tonight, odd flares of emotion stirred in him.

Emotion was dangerous. It could ensnare a man, mess up his concentration and make him careless. Dawn Ericson was nothing more than a fantasy. That was all she'd ever be to him. Period.

But she had been beautiful.

Restless, he dressed and headed for town—or what there was of it. The mountain community consisted of a main street and one parallel side street, plus four or five cross streets. He stopped at a barber shop before searching out a place for dinner. Later, following the friendly barber's instructions, he drove along a cross street that wound over to Honey Lake.

A county road skirted the lake on this side. Vacation cabins dotted the scrubby woodland to his left. The setting sun gleamed off the calm lake surface to his right, painting a shimmering path of gold and pink on the water. Smoke wafted from the chimney of a steakhouse, broadcasting its wares to the hungry traveler.

He sniffed appreciatively as he climbed down from his truck. Hunger gnawed at him. Hearing laughter as he stepped inside the rustic building, he admitted to another hunger—one that couldn't be satisfied with a thick steak and fries. He cursed as eyes as translucent as moonstone crinkled and smiled at him. Shaking the vision off, he crossed the room.

Ignoring the laughing foursome at a booth, he chose the last table by the window where he could sit with his back to the wall and gaze at the lake. When the waitress came, he ordered without looking at the menu.

Alone again, he contemplated the deepening twilight and thought of tomorrow and what it would bring. A man needed to be prepared for whatever might happen when he entered enemy territory. That was why he'd scouted it out beforehand.

Across the way, a tall slim woman came out of the local market, crossed the street and tossed her purchases in an oversize pickup. His heart lurched, then righted itself when she glanced his way. Their eyes met.

He saw her hand fly to the snug harbor between her breasts and knew, if he touched her where her hand rested, he'd feel a heartbeat as furious as his own. Impulsively, he waved his hand toward the seat opposite him, inviting her to join him.

She shook her head.

Shrugging, he tossed the rejection off. It was what he'd expected. She turned her head as if hearing someone call to her. The wind tangled her hair about her shoulders. Her long skirt swirled around her ankles and caressed her hips and abdomen. Hunger ate at him.

A long shadow cast by the setting sun heralded another person's arrival on the scene. Hunter McLean strode up, his own package dangling from his hand.

The rancher spoke to Dawn, then held the passenger door open for her to climb in. He patted her bottom, then laughed when she slapped his hand away.

Jackson controlled the anger that made him want to walk outside and smash a fist into McLean's mouth.

When she glanced his way again, he deliberately gave her a knowing smile. She didn't respond. Instead, she continued to watch him, her expression solemn, while her escort walked around the truck, climbed in and drove off.

When they were gone, he slouched in the chair as if the stuffing in his backbone had run out. Fatigue washed over him, displacing the anger. He felt the cold of the mountain air seep through the glass and surround him.

A lone woman entered the restaurant. She chose a table where he could see her and she could watch him. When their eyes met, she smiled a tentative greeting.

He recognized her loneliness and knew she would welcome his companionship for more than just a meal. At times in the past, when the need to connect with another human had been too much, he'd accepted invitations like the one just offered.

Tonight he wouldn't. Glancing at a patch of light blue sky that lingered in the sunset, he thought it might be a long time before he could turn to a woman for easy pleasure again. It unnerved him when eyes as mysterious as moonstone seemed to smile at him from some secret inner place.

Jackson slid out of the truck and glanced around. The hair on the back of his neck prickled, alerting him to danger. This was where he'd met disaster once before. He'd been carted off, his body bruised, one eye swollen shut and his nose bloody. At Hunter McLean's orders two cowboys had dumped him at the highway like a sack of trash.

That wouldn't happen again.

He turned at the sound of a car. A dark sedan stopped and a lawyer climbed out. Jackson could spot one a mile away by the way they moved.

"I'm Sam Norris, attorney for the McLeans." The man held out his hand. "Well, for John and now Margaret and Hunter," he corrected with a forthright smile, obviously remembering that Jackson had asked his own attorney to represent him at the probate hearing. "You must be Jackson."

"That's right." Jackson shook hands with the man.

"John and I grew up together. Your father was a straight arrow, as honest as they come."

Jackson recoiled from the statement. "He wasn't honest with my mother or with me."

"She knew his circumstances." Sam shook his head sadly. "John fell in love. I told him it was madness—" He broke off, then sighed. "Love's a messy business. No law can overrule the heart."

Jackson snorted at the mention of love and bit back the scornful retort that sprang to his tongue. He didn't give a damn about his father or his love life. He was here for one reason—revenge. Let McLean try to throw him off the place this time. He smiled, thinking of the satisfaction he'd get, knowing the other man was powerless.

A picture sprang to mind. Hair like silver, eyes like the sky. A faint reprimand in the calm, direct stare. He mentally returned the look, then glanced down the road, wondering where she was.

No, he wasn't there to see *her*.

A treacherous thought came to mind. The woman had been attracted to him—or at least, to the savage she'd found in the woods. It would be a nice irony to steal her away from the other son. His smile felt hard-edged, even to him.

"We're expected," the attorney interrupted his musing and led the way up the sidewalk to the front door.

The housekeeper opened it before they had time to pound the brass knocker mounted on the solid oak. A scene depicting a cowboy on a horse, roping a bull, was carved into the hardwood. He remembered it from his earlier visit. The view had been different when he'd been sprawled on his back on the wide porch, blood running from his nose, his pride as tattered as his jeans, as he was beaten to the ground by the then twenty-year-old Hunter McLean.

He forced the memory back and ran a hand through his short hair. He felt odd with his neck bare. Exposed. Vulnerable. Like Samson must have felt after Delilah did him in. A woman could be just as dangerous as a man when it came to being enemies.

"Hello, Mr. Norris, please come in." The housekeeper's gaze took in both men. "The family is in the den."

Jackson forced himself to breathe slowly and deeply. He had a right to be here. This time they couldn't throw him out. He owned half of the place.

He entered behind the lawyer, then stepped to one side for a quick survey of the room. The widow sat in her wheelchair as usual. McLean stood beside her with his hands thrust into his hip pockets. He looked big and mean.

Mrs. Ericson sat in a padded chair close to her best friend. He thought of asking why Dawn wasn't there to present a solid front and defend the home against his invasion, too, but didn't.

"Coffee?" the housekeeper asked.

Anna Hamilton was her name. Russell's wife. Russell was the foreman. Larry was their son. Jackson associated the names with the people he knew to be on the ranch. It was wise to know the enemy.

"No, thanks." He wanted his hands free, just in case.

"We won't poison you," McLean remarked, his green eyes with the gold flecks eerily familiar.

Jackson returned the cold smile.

The attorney took a seat and accepted a cup of coffee from the housekeeper, who silently left the room after a sympathetic glance at Mrs. McLean.

"I should go," Dawn's mother murmured.

"No, stay," her friend requested. "I really don't see that we have anything to discuss with this…this person." She may have looked refined, but her voice had the cutting edge of a buzz saw. That she looked upon him as pure dirt was no secret.

He mentally shrugged. He'd been treated worse.

"Now, Margaret," her lawyer chided gently. "We have to arrange the ranching accounts. I suggested, and John agreed to the idea, that the ranch pay Hunter and…Jackson a salary commensurate with the foreman's pay. Net profit on the ranch is to be split between the three of you at year's end. The other holdings go equally to the two sons."

Jackson didn't miss the slight hesitation before his name was coupled with Hunter's, also the fact that the mother's face paled at the mention of *two* sons. He met her furious glance steadily. She looked away as if she couldn't stand the sight of him.

So okay, he hadn't expected them to greet him with open arms. He could handle hatred and whatever else they chose to dish out.

"Where will he live?" she asked the other two men. "He isn't staying in this house."

There was an awkward silence—an admission that Jackson had the right if he so chose.

"Isn't the house part of the ranch?" he inquired, keeping his tone polite. He wasn't going to fight with the McLeans, but he wasn't going to be pushed around, either.

He looked at the lawyer, who nodded.

McLean briefly laid a protective hand on his mother's shoulder. "This is my mother's house. It was built for her. You stay on the ranch, you stay in the bunkhouse."

"Why do we have to allow him here?" the widow

protested. "It was my money that saved the ranch. John would have lost it if my father hadn't signed the papers—"

"It was a loan," Sam interrupted before she could disclose more of the intimate family history.

Jackson wondered if his father had married her to save the ranch. Nothing the man had done would surprise him at this point. "There's a cabin in the woods on the other side of the horse paddock," he told them. "It's empty. I'll live there."

"For how long?" McLean interjected.

"Until I decide differently." Jackson shifted his stance, ready to defend himself as anger flashed in the other man's eyes. His brother. Yeah, right.

But the thought didn't amuse him.

He wasn't even sure why he was here. Curiosity? A need to force his presence on them after that other visit? He certainly didn't give a damn about his father's money.

Once, he would have given an arm to be included with this family on this ranch. When he'd found out he was the bastard son, he'd gone through a period of hating his mother. Not his father, but the woman who had given birth to him and had been there for him all his life.

He'd hated her for not being this refined, fair-skinned, blue-eyed mother whose son had a right to live with his father. It was only later, as he grew into manhood, that he'd come to hate the man who had abandoned them, except for a monthly check—conscience money, he figured—and forgiven his mother for loving the SOB.

But he'd never accepted another cent from his father after he'd been thrown off the ranch. He'd gotten his diploma from the boarding school and headed back to the reservation where he'd raised horses and crafted jewelry for tourists.

"The cabin doesn't have electricity," Hunter said.

"I'll fix it up."

"Fine," the attorney inserted into the conversation. "That sounds like just the thing."

"Have you ever worked a ranch before?" Hunter demanded.

"I was born on one—not a big one like you have here, but we had cows and horses. Sheep, too. My grandfather had a spread on the reservation."

Twin dots of color splashed Mrs. McLean's cheeks as he threw his background in their faces. He wasn't going to hide his heritage. He was what he was.

He ran a hand behind his neck, feeling the short hairs on his nape, and wondered why he'd had it cut. Then he remembered. He'd wanted to look civilized. For *her,* the woman who was coming up the walk at that moment. He watched from the window until she disappeared up the porch steps.

She knocked, then opened the door. "Hi," she said, entering the den with her leggy stride. "Am I late for lunch? Anna called and said I was to come up."

She brought the outdoors with her—the warmth of sunshine, the breeziness of the June day, the scent of the herbs she worked with. A sprig of lavender was poking through the buttonhole of her shirt.

Her skirt was long and pleated, the material

splashed in swirls of bright blue, pink, lavender and green. He thought of lying in a field of wildflowers with her, of stroking skin as delicate as a squash-blossom petal. His heart kicked around in his chest before quieting down.

"No, you're just in time," Anna assured her, appearing in the hallway, a guilty flush highlighting her smile.

In time to save them? He wondered how often Dawn had been called upon to perform the role of peacemaker in this family. He stilled a sardonic lift of his lips at the thought of this sylph of a woman saving him and McLean from a brawl, and relaxed slightly.

Anna looked at Mrs. McLean. "Lunch is ready."

Jackson had to give the older woman credit. She nodded with a cool composure at odds with the anger in her eyes. "We'll continue this discussion after lunch."

During the brief silence after this announcement, everyone looked at him to gauge his reaction. For a moment he remembered being seventeen and unwanted in this house. He shoved the memory into the past with a savage curse.

Dawn came to him and held out her hand. "I'm Dawn. You must be Jackson." Her eyes acknowledged their meeting in the woods. She appeared troubled by their shared secret.

"Yes." He took her hand and held it for a few seconds. He looked at the small calluses across her palm. She must often forget to wear gloves when she worked with the horses. He imagined her mother fussing at her about it.

She removed her hand from his when his hold on her grew too long. He stepped away, angry with himself for clinging like a kid. He didn't need anyone—hadn't since he was seventeen and his mother had died, forgotten by the man she'd loved and trusted.

He thought of asking Dawn if she'd like to join him up on the mountain again, but refrained. To throw their ''secret'' meeting into McLean's face would be a petty revenge on his part. A reference to their previous meal together would stir up questions she probably didn't want to answer, and he was oddly reluctant to cause her any embarrassment, no matter how sweet it might be to get one up on Hunter and his hatchet-faced mother.

Yeah, he knew why Anna had called. The situation needed defusing. Mrs. McLean and Dawn's mother were openly disdainful. His half brother was ready to defend his home turf. As for himself, he knew how he felt.

His stance was belligerent, ready for action if McLean wanted to start anything. The chip on the other man's shoulder was all but visible to the naked eye. Jackson figured it was the same with himself.

''Let's not keep Anna waiting,'' Dawn said brightly. ''Sam, are you joining us? Anna said we're having that tuna aspic you like so well.''

The lawyer did his best to ease the situation. ''That Anna. I've been trying to hire her away for years—''

''I have not invited *him* to join us,'' Mrs. McLean interrupted, her face once more flaming with anger.

Jackson nodded toward the door. "I'll take my chances with the bunkhouse grub or at the greasy spoon down the highway." He met Margaret's glare with a lazy grin guaranteed to drive an enemy into a rage. "Never been poisoned by either one yet," he drawled.

Hunter stepped forward, his fists clenched. "On this ranch, we don't poison vermin. We just shoot 'em when they show their ugly faces around here."

"Yeah? I'll keep an eye out. One thing we had on the res was rattlers. We did target practice on 'em."

"A born killer," Mrs. McLean said, her voice shaking as if she expected him to pull out a six-shooter and drill them all on the spot. "You put me in this wheelchair. You and your mother."

Every cell in his body froze. What the hell was the woman talking about? The others looked as stunned as he felt. They stood frozen in place, posed like ice sculptures at a winter carnival.

"Sixteen years ago I found out about John's... other family. I was going to leave him, but the roads were wet and icy in spots. The car skidded and hit a bridge. I was left like this." She gestured bitterly toward her useless legs, then stared at Jackson with helpless fury. "Because of you and your mother."

The silence writhed around them like snakes in a pit before he moved.

"Wait," Dawn said, but he ignored her.

In three strides, he was out of there.

Chapter Three

"Tired?"

Dawn roused from her musing to answer Hunter. "Not really. Just thinking."

She leaned on the railing around the horse paddock. The black stallion belonging to Jackson Firebird grazed along the fence. Hunter held his son on his shoulders. J.J. watched the horse.

At nearly three, the child still didn't speak. He'd also been slow to crawl and walk. When the cattle truck had overturned with Dawn's father and sister inside, J.J. had been fourteen months old. Since his mother's death, he had withdrawn into himself, his eyes wary as he watched the world with distrust and a child's inexpressible sense of tragedy. The accident had been twenty-one months ago—a time of unbearable grief. It still echoed through their lives.

From the cabin set on a knoll above the paddock, she heard the steady *whap* of a hammer. During the past two weeks, Jackson had worked on his home from first light until dark. He was building an addition to the cabin.

As a kid, she'd played with her dolls there. The place had been a playhouse, a cave, a pirate ship and, during her teenage years, a refuge. It held special memories for her.

"Thinking about us?" Hunter asked casually. He held his son's ankles and stared up at the twilight sky. He looked tired. It had been an uneasy two weeks on the ranch.

A meeting between the two brothers had resulted in Hunter running the ranch and Jackson taking over the logging operation. He'd stopped the clear-cutting and told the logging company to vacate when their contract ended.

She gazed at the few stars that had appeared with a pang of guilt. She hadn't been thinking of Hunter. In spite of her good sense, which told her to avoid Jackson, she found herself looking for him, listening for the sound of his pickup when he went in and out on the ranch road.

Hunter was her best friend. The mothers wanted them to marry. J.J. needed a mother; Hunter needed a wife.

She leaned her head on her crossed arms and studied him, this man she'd known since birth. Close to thirty-one, he was five and a half years older than her own twenty-five years. He was as tall as his half brother. Once, he'd been a gentler man than he was now.

Hunter had let her tag after him during their growing years until he'd reached high school and started dating. Then he'd gone off to college where he'd became engaged for a short time. That hadn't worked out. When he'd returned to the ranch, he'd taken over its operations while his father handled the investments and logging contracts.

She'd left for UC-Davis the following year, spending five happy years studying and getting a master's degree in ranch management. In the meantime, Hunter and her sister April, who had been four years her senior, had married and started a family. Dawn had been thrilled for them.

Upon returning home, she'd started her own horse boarding and training business—a dream come true.

The accident that had taken April and their father had happened the same year. She and Hunter had shared so much since then—the awful tragedy, the care of his son—but eventually less serious matters— the reasons for the breakup of his first engagement, her crush on a high-school quarterback that had ended badly, a tepid involvement with a college chum. They had discovered each other as adults rather than the kids who had known each other "forever." They had become friends.

Three months ago, his father had died of a heart attack. Dawn had called the medics and administered CPR while the housekeeper ran to find Hunter and bring him to the house. She'd stayed with him at the hospital and through the funeral. That was when their friendship had changed.

Hunter wanted more. He needed a family, mostly for his son—a fact that didn't particularly bother Dawn. He was woven so thoroughly into the fabric of her days, she couldn't imagine life without him. She loved him. Of course she did. But was she *in* love with him?

A face came to her in the deepening twilight. Jackson Firebird seemed to be watching her with that mocking half smile that was so intriguing. She shivered as if the cool night wind had invaded her soul.

Hunter tossed the jacket he carried over her shoulders. "That will warm you up. Or we can take J.J. to the house and I'll warm you in other ways."

His amused suggestion warred with the worry that plagued her. "Hunter," she began, then hesitated.

"What's bothering you, sweet pea?" he asked, using her father's old pet name. "You've been quiet for days. Did you have a spat with your mother?"

"No. It's nothing like that. I…"

The pounding from the cabin abruptly stopped as if Jackson had paused to listen, too. Her gaze was drawn in that direction. She spotted his lanky outline on the porch, more a shadow against shadows than substance. He raised his hand and gave her a lazy wave, knowing she was watching.

After a moment, when she didn't return his greeting, he went inside the cabin.

An ominous frown settled across Hunter's handsome face. "He's enlarging the cabin. I suppose he plans to be here for the long haul. He's been watching how things are run on the ranch, too.''

She hadn't told him that Jackson had been in the area for over a week before he'd appeared at the ranch. Guilt nibbled at her conscience. She'd promised to keep his secret and really, there was nothing to tell. She'd come upon the man in the woods. Nothing had happened.

So why couldn't she talk about it?

''I read a newspaper article about him. There was a picture with it. He learned silver crafting from his grandfather, who apparently was rather well-known for his designs. Two years ago, he won a DeBeers international design award. Last Christmas there was an exclusive showing of his one-of-a-kind diamond pieces at Tiffany.''

''He must be doing well.'' The tone was cynical.

''What are you going to do if he decides to live here all the time?''

''I know what I'd like to do.''

''Throw him off the place?''

''You got it. I did, once. He came to the ranch and upset Mom. He wouldn't believe her when she said Dad was out of town. When he said John McLean was his father, I thought he was lying.''

Dawn gasped and pressed a hand between her breasts. A shivery pain flashed through her. ''When?''

''Eleven years ago. I was home for spring break. Dad had given me the quarter-horse stud I wanted to improve the ranch stock. I was in the paddock working with him.''

She knew from the McLean attorney that Jackson

was twenty-eight. So he'd been seventeen when he'd come looking for his father. She wondered if her mother knew of the episode. Probably. The two women confided everything.

Why hadn't anyone told her? Because eleven years ago, she'd been all of fourteen. Too young for adult things.

But Jackson had only been seventeen.

"Dad had gone down to Sacramento to protest some new bit of legislation. This guy showed up the next day, demanding to see his father."

Dawn's heart ached at the harsh bitterness in Hunter's tone. The father had hurt both his sons. "What happened?"

"We fought. After I had a couple of ranch hands cart him off the place Mom told me the boy had lied. When I asked my father, he said it was all a mistake. He said he'd known them a long time ago and had helped them out with money a few times, but the boy had misunderstood what his mother had told him. When the will was read—" Hunter broke off as anger and grief thickened his voice.

Dawn waited quietly.

"It turns out my father was the one who'd lied to us all those years. He'd had another family all along."

She squeezed his arm in sympathy. He'd come to her afterward, still in shock that he had a brother and that the other son now owned half the ranch that Hunter loved. He'd railed against the father he'd always admired. It had been a cruel blow.

At that time she'd thought John McLean had a lot to answer for. After meeting Jackson, she realized it was even more than she'd thought. He'd hurt another son and another woman just as deeply, just as cruelly.

She shivered again. "So much pain."

"If he causes my mother any grief, he'll be off the place so fast he won't know what hit him," Hunter stated in a deadly snarl.

"You can't fight with him this time. He has a right to be here."

Hunter snorted belligerently. After a bit he sighed and caught her hand in his, then held it for the rest of their walk until they turned toward the road shared by the two ranches. The McLean spread dwarfed the Ericson holdings by ten acres to each one of hers.

They returned to his house where she bathed J.J. and put him to bed. She read a story to the solemn child, her heart overflowing with love for him.

Later, Hunter walked her home. At her driveway, he pulled her into his arms. Instinctively she turned her head from a kiss that would have been filled with anger and frustration, not with love and passion, over a situation he could do nothing to control.

Dawn held him and made soothing sounds. At last, the rigid muscles across his shoulders relaxed.

"Sorry," he whispered.

"It's okay," she assured him. She rubbed the frown lines from his face.

He slipped a hand into her hair and kissed her several times on the temple, his lips gentle. He stroked through her hair and removed the clasp at the back of her head that held the top and sides away from her face.

"I love your hair," he said. "It always smells like

something spicy and sweet, good enough to eat.'' He chuckled as the last of the anger dissolved.

''Hunter, do you love me?'' she heard herself ask and was surprised by the question.

''Of course,'' he stated with masculine arrogance. ''I've asked you to marry me, haven't I?''

She thought about it. She couldn't remember if he'd actually said the words. ''No, I think you told me I should think about setting the date,'' she said, trying for a lighter note.

''God, what a blunder.'' He groaned, chuckled, then kissed her in the vicinity of her ear. ''Will you?''

Her hesitation was palpable. ''Are we in love?'' she asked finally.

He lifted his head. She sensed his heavy frown and impatient glare. The tension returned with a tightening of his shoulder muscles beneath her hands. ''If you have to ask, maybe the answer is no.''

She sighed, then leaned forward and kissed him softly on the mouth. ''Maybe we both need more time to think things through. Life has been difficult the past three months. We don't want to make any more mistakes.''

While she knew much about Hunter's life, his hopes and his dreams, she hadn't known about the other McLean son. No one had told her of that visit long ago. She wondered why Hunter had never mentioned it during the times they'd talked about everything else. Until the reading of the will, Jackson's existence had been ignored.

She felt a terrible ache in her heart for the younger son. He'd been alone for years. Guilt followed on the heels of that thought. It was Hunter she had to think about. He was her lifelong neighbor and friend.

And her love?

"Mistakes," he repeated harshly. "Yeah, there have been enough of those in the family."

"Let's think carefully before we decide the future, okay?" She patted his lean jaw, said good-night, then slipped away from him. Inside the house, she waved before closing the door.

"Was that Hunter with you?" her mother asked, looking up from the television program.

"Yes. We went for a walk. Mom, did you know about Jackson McLean, about when he came here eleven years ago?"

Mrs. Ericson shook her head. "I was as shocked as the rest of the county when the will was read. Margaret never breathed a word about John's other family."

Dawn thought of the shock the other woman must have gone through—finding out her husband was unfaithful, then having a wreck that crippled her for life. She sighed in pity for all of them—Margaret and Hunter and Jackson, and Jackson's mother, too.

"Why is he staying here?" her mother asked. It was a rhetorical question. "It can only cause trouble."

"All people want to discover their roots. Maybe Jackson does, too."

Her mother's gaze sharpened as she studied Dawn. "Don't go feeling sorry for him," she warned. "You always were bad about taking up causes. Remember those vagrants who stopped here that time? You just had to befriend the little girl. You ended up with a headful of lice and the French doll Margaret gave you went missing.''

Dawn smiled and headed for her room. ''That was a learning experience,'' she agreed, remembering her bitter disappointment in her new friend. ''I'm going to change, then read a while before turning in. Good night, Mom.''

In her room, she left the light off after closing the door. Going to the window, she looked at the light blinking through the shifting foliage of the trees. She had to admit, Jackson Firebird McLean had a hold on her imagination and wouldn't let go.

And yes, her heart ached for the seventeen-year-old who'd come to find his father and had found another son and a hostile wife instead. The shock of discovery must have been devastating on both sides.

She shook her head over her musings as she slipped into the extra-large T-shirt she slept in. Her mother was right. She tended to be softhearted. Which could equate to softheadedness at times. She was too quick to sympathize. She'd been wrong about people in the past.

Maybe Jackson had known what a stir his presence would make eleven years ago and hadn't cared. Maybe he'd wanted to cause trouble. People could be like that.

And maybe she'd better stop thinking about him. She had her future to consider—hers and Hunter's and J.J.'s.

After washing up, she lay under the sheet and watched the scene outside the window. From here, she could see the lights of the ranch house, and, farther up in the woods, the flickering light of the cabin through the trees.

She looked at that light for a long time, then realized what she was doing. Guilt tore at her.

Jackson stopped the truck on the side of the road and climbed down. He found Dawn bending over a table of herbs in one of the greenhouses, pulling flower heads.

"You'll never get seeds if you keep doing that."

She spun around. Her hand flew to that harbor between her breasts that he wanted to explore. Her breath seemed to catch, then she smiled uneasily. Her gaze flicked up the road to the ranch house.

"Worried that Hunter might see us?" he asked, letting her see the cynicism in his smile.

"I don't know."

Her candor was like a kick on the shin. It got his attention. He watched her pull a few more flowers off. Her hands trembled—not much, but enough.

He sensed the tension between them. It wound around them like a spider spinning a golden thread of promise. Dawn, the beginning of light. He thought of spending the night with her in his arms.

While his physical reaction to the idea was predictable and totally normal, he frowned as other emotions swirled through him. He was here to claim his rights as a lawful, although illegitimate, heir. He'd realized he didn't need revenge on McLean. His very presence took care of that.

"I'm having a housewarming dinner tonight. You want to come?" he asked.

She shook her head.

"Afraid?"

"Maybe. There's something hard and calculating about you. I don't like it. The savage was more compassionate."

She saw and understood too much, this woman who sang as she worked.

Regret sprang up. He was surprised at the impulse. Something about her made him go soft in the head so that he wanted to forget the desire to disrupt McLean's easy life. He wanted to apologize for thinking of using her for that purpose.

He clamped his teeth together. The McLeans deserved a little crinkle in the smooth fabric of their days.

This woman was *their* friend. Like the store owners in the small town who looked upon him as an outsider, so did she. He made her nervous. She thought of him as a savage who would pounce on her without a warning. Regret hit him again, confusing him, making him angry.

She looked at him, catching him off guard, his feelings exposed. He forced a cynical smile.

"Someday you'll eat with me again," he announced in a low tone, deliberately layering his prediction with a touch of mystery and danger.

He saw her swallow and wondered what words she wanted to say. Someday she'd whisper soft words, lover's words, in his ears. Before the summer was over, he promised himself.

His blood thrummed wildly through his body. He turned and loped back to the safety of the truck before he made a fool of himself. It was she who would quiver with desire. He would win her—the woman with hair like silver and eyes like the sky—and then laugh at his brother's loss.

Dawn wakened as the first light of early morning played over her face. She yawned and snuggled under the covers, her thoughts wandering to the night and dreams she couldn't remember, but whose haunting quality bothered her.

Getting up, she dressed in a matching skirt and top and slipped on a sweater. Hunter was having some friends over for a cookout that afternoon and she'd promised to help him.

In a few minutes, nibbling on a piece of toast, she went outside and looked over the orderly rows of plants in the fields. The Ericson Nursery was known for organic gardening. It worked very well for her and her mom.

Beyond the greenhouses where they raised the more delicate herbs, the white-faced Herefords grazed or stared solemnly at the hills as if contemplating nature.

Peace surrounded her. She liked Sunday mornings better than any other time. She had the place to herself. After petting and checking the horses she was boarding, she turned and crossed the road.

The woods were cool, the warmth of the sun not yet penetrating the foliage. She wrapped her arms across her middle and climbed the winding, barely discernible path up the side of the mountain.

At one point she came to a fork. One way led upward to the place where she'd met the "outsider" preparing his lunch over the fire. The other...

Her breath quickened as she took the lower trail—the one that led to the cabin where she used to play house with her dolls. She tried to recall if there had been an imaginary father in her mother role, but she hadn't thought that far ahead in those days.

She stopped in the shadow of a pine and looked at the house. Jackson sat on the repaired porch, a cup of steaming coffee in his hand, his eyes on the horizon.

He ignored her as she crossed the unmowed grass and joined him. She climbed the two steps and settled beside his sinewy frame, awareness in every cell of her body.

"Good morning."

He gave a sound of acknowledgment, more a snort than a greeting. He acted more reserved with her this morning, his attitude not as sardonic as it had been yesterday when he'd invited her to dine here with him, his hunger blatant in his snug jeans.

Heat burned through her. The intensity of it alarmed her as much as the intensity she sometimes sensed in him. His power to hurt those she loved worried her. But her reaction to him—their enemy—was even more dangerous.

With her feet on the second step, she propped her elbows on her knees and her chin in her hands and watched as the sun highlighted a tall peak still white with snow before climbing the mountain's steep shoulder and peeking into the valley.

One of the warm rays delved into his eyes when he finally turned his head toward her. Iridescent green gleamed briefly at her, enchantingly elusive....

"Fox fire," she murmured. "Usually seen in the woods only at night."

Russ had told her about it long ago when she'd asked. "Fairy dust," he'd said. "If you touch it, you'll become enslaved to the fairy who left it behind. That's why mortals should stay out of the woods. Fairies especially like children."

A chill raced along her neck as it had when she'd been eight and the foreman had warned her about playing alone in the woods. But even then she'd known it wasn't the woods that boded ill. The hazards were all too human.

She glanced at the silent man beside her. He watched her without a change in expression, his eyes opaque and emotionless.

"Good morning," she said again. "Yes, I'm fine. Thank you for asking. And you?"

His expression was mocking. "I'm not feeling very sociable right now."

"When will you be? An hour from now? Tomorrow? Should I come back then?"

The sun rose completely above the horizon. His eyes and his mood seemed to grow darker. "I'll send you an invitation when I want company."

"I won't hold my breath." She smiled at his scowl. "What were you thinking before I barged in uninvited? You looked solemn."

''That I like being alone. Life is peaceful that way.'' The lethal glance he gave her was a warning not to push too far. ''I'm the enemy. I eat skinny gals like you for a snack.''

She spoke the first unguarded thought that flitted through her mind. ''I might bite, too.''

The next thing she knew she was flat on her back, one savage warrior leaning over her, pinning her hands beside her head on the rough planks.

''What do you want from me?'' he demanded, his mouth inches from hers. ''A little thrill on the side before you settle into wedded bliss with my *brother?*'' He spat the word at her, a reminder of the unbridgeable distance between them, and that they were enemies.

''Hunter and I aren't planning marriage.''

''People in town say you are.'' His mouth was a little closer.

''Hunter and I haven't said that.''

''If you play your cards right, he'll ask you. You can use me to make him jealous. Maybe that's what you're doing up here now.''

''Or maybe I figure if I can't get him, I'll latch on to the other heir.'' She returned his glare until he laughed sardonically and the harshness in his gaze lessened.

''Right, I'm a real catch.''

She thought about his hands, the strength in them, the way he held her pinned without hurting her or even making her feel threatened physically.

An odd sort of trust—to feel secure with so fierce a warrior, one with so much anger in his heart.

"Why did you cut your hair?" she asked when he moved back and let her up. She reached out and touched the short strands. His hair was slightly damp. She wondered if he'd bathed in the creek again. There was no water in the cabin.

"Because."

She waited.

"I decided I'd go for the civilized look. The era of the noble savage is over, I've been told."

She gave him an oblique glance, then studied the colors of the sunrise. "I liked him. He was…" She couldn't think of the proper word.

"He was a man who hadn't been around a woman in a long time," he informed her. "I'd hoped you'd want to play for a while."

She wondered if he'd been "around" a woman since she'd left him on the mountain seventeen days ago. A stab of emotion, too brief to define, shot along her nerves. She wondered if he had stayed at the local motel while he was becoming civilized. The suit he'd worn at the McLean house had been expensive. His boots had been handcrafted.

Dressed like that, he appeared to be what he evidently was—a highly successful person, wealthy, cosmopolitan and assured. A man women would try to attract.

But he'd been alone at the restaurant.

She relaxed. "Did you find someone to join you for dinner at the restaurant that night?"

He hesitated, then shook his head. "I wasn't looking for company."

She didn't point out that he'd indicated she would be welcome at his table.

"What are you looking for?" she inquired softly. "It isn't part of the will that you have to live here—especially like this." She indicated the rustic cabin.

"I wanted to check out my inheritance and make sure the McLeans didn't try to cheat me out of my share."

"Hunter wouldn't do that," she said. "You'll have to give them time. Hunter is fair-minded, but he's angry now and still in shock. Margaret will never like you. You're a constant reminder that her husband was unfaithful to her."

His expression turned sardonic. "Yeah, the old man was as much of a bastard as I am."

"Stop it," she ordered, as fierce as he in her anger. "That's an outmoded idea in this day and age. You are what you make of yourself. But you're going to have to back off and understand what others are going thr—"

He stood and glared down at her. "I don't need a lecture. I learned all the lessons in life I needed by the time I was seventeen, so forget it."

"When you came to the ranch to see your father, why did you come?" She spoke her conclusion aloud: "Were you going to confront him in front of his family?"

"I wanted him to come home. My mother was dying and she wanted him, the devil knows why. He hadn't been around in years, not since I was twelve. He suddenly stopped coming one day." He glared as if it were her fault.

"Because his wife was permanently injured trying to leave him," Dawn said, seeing the whole picture—discovery of the betrayal, the hurt and anger, accusations, Margaret's accident, guilt, wasted lives. "Is that when you discovered he had a wife and son?"

"No, not then. When I was fourteen, I saw a check from my father and demanded to know why he never came around. My mother thought I was old enough to know the truth, so she told me. Before, when I'd asked about his absences, she'd said he was a very busy man. Yeah, he was."

"John must have loved your mother very much. He wasn't the type to live easily with deception."

"He was a liar who took what he wanted without giving a damn about anything else." He strode into the cabin.

Dawn leaned against the post so she could watch him as he prepared his breakfast. He opened a can of corned-beef hash, dumped it into a skillet and turned the burner on.

"You staying?" he asked.

"No, my mom will be expecting me." She stood and dusted off her backside. For a moment, she had the most insane impulse to invite him to Hunter's cookout.

Turning, she caught his eyes on her. They watched each other warily, desire springing to life between them. He moved his lips slightly, as if readying for a kiss.

For a wild, delicious moment, she wondered what it would be like, his kiss. To have the freedom to touch each other. Intimately. Without asking.

A horn blared. In the valley, she saw a pickup at the bunkhouse. One of the hands came out and climbed in. She looked back at Jackson.

His face had hardened and he looked the fierce warrior ready for war.

"You're here for revenge," she murmured, knowing it was true. It make her sad for reasons she couldn't name.

His expression smoothed. "What makes you think that? I have everything I ever dreamed of—an impressive spread, money to spend, a beautiful woman at my door. What more could a man want?"

She shook her head, her emotions in a welter. "You have a right to be angry with your father. So does Hunter. But not with each other. None of this was of your making, either of you."

He flipped the hash over to brown on the other side. "Don't go feeling sorry for me," he ordered. He sliced two pieces of bread from a crusty loaf. After he tilted the hash onto a plate, he broke two eggs into the skillet.

"I don't." She stepped off the porch, leaving him alone with his breakfast in the cabin he was fixing up with the sole intent to defy Margaret and Hunter and the father he wanted to hate.

"'Ladybug, ladybug, fly away home....'"

The mocking words drifted to her through the open door, but he didn't protest her leaving. When she looked back, he stood on the porch, a plate in his hand.

The chill of the woods reached out and enclosed her. All the way down the path, she considered that final image of him in the cabin doorway and thought of his being alone as he'd been for the eleven years since his mother's death.

She pressed a hand to her heart. She wouldn't be soft toward him. He was a heartache waiting to happen to some unwary woman. That woman wouldn't be her.

Chapter Four

Jackson woke feeling edgy and rough. He recalled it was Sunday morning. Dawn and her mother and the McLeans would dress up and drive down to Litchfield for church, then stay for lunch, assuming they followed the pattern of the two prior Sabbaths. They wouldn't arrive home until two.

He rose, washed up in a basin, then grimaced as he flung the water outside. Tomorrow, the company he'd hired would run a pipe from the water main going to the ranch up to the cabin. A septic tank would also be installed. He had a hot-water heater on order at the local hardware store.

Soon his home would be as modern as the ranch house. And he'd be as civilized as his brother. The thought drew a harsh bark of laughter. If he stayed there a hundred years, he wouldn't be the equivalent to McLean in the eyes of the local people. He could sense their suspicion each time he put in an order.

There was only one person whose manner was welcoming, who didn't seem to think he might revert to type and scalp her if she made him angry. He dressed quickly in the morning chill while eyes as gentle as the first light of morning seemed to smile at him.

Shaking off the image, he ate a bowl of cereal, then headed for the stable, restlessness eating at him.

He had hardly ridden the stallion since bringing it down from the mountain pasture where he'd camped. He'd go for a long ride up in the hills, commune with nature and all that, and check on the logging operations.

The black whuffled a greeting when Jackson entered the stall and playfully butted him. Jackson gave the horse a good scratching around the ears, then pushed the horse's nose aside in order to dump a bucket of oats into the bin.

Snorting gustily, the stallion ate while Jackson leaned against the rough planking and thought of things he knew he should put out of his mind—such as asking Dawn to join him.

He had observed her working with the horses she trained, her manner relaxed and sure. She was good.

Restlessness hit him again. He went outside, leaving the door open so the black could join him, and watched the sky gradually lighten. A light came on over at the foreman's house, another at the bunkhouse where the hands lived.

In the summer, there were constant chores to be done on a ranch. McLean put up his own hay for winter feed, so there was mowing and baling to do. The ranch had a contract with the county to mow the verge of the main roads in their area. That was another source of income and a few more bales of hay, too. The JMc was an efficient operation.

When a light appeared at the main house, he turned toward it. From a window on the lower floor, he saw Margaret McLean watching him through the French doors leading onto the patio from her bedroom. He tipped his hat politely, not expecting a return greeting. In the three weeks since his arrival, she'd never once acknowledged him.

She continued to stare at him with a set, unreadable expression just as he'd expected. He smiled grimly. An enemy should never be predictable.

He turned and surveyed the ranch, wondering how she saw the place now that she wasn't an official owner. He'd learned there had been a prenuptial agreement, drawn up by her father, so McLean couldn't make use of his wife's money if the ranch failed. Each partner had retained the portion he or she had brought into the marriage, thus the ranch had been solely the old man's to will wherever he would. There was a certain ironic justice in that.

But the fact that she'd been left out, except for a third of the ranch's yearly earnings, must have been a harsh final blow from a husband who'd been in love with another woman most of their married life, if the McLean attorney and Dawn were to be believed.

He remembered how it had felt to discover his father had another family. There had been pain and a sense of betrayal. His mother had known her lover was married. She'd accepted him on that basis. Margaret had found out the hard way—just as he had.

Not that he felt sorry for her. The woman had lived in the lap of luxury all her life with hardly a ripple. Until the accident that had crippled her.

She'd been given a pretty tough hand to play in that deal, he had to admit. He'd hate to be confined to a wheelchair. Russ had said Margaret was once an expert rider with the sure hands of a born horsewoman.

He shook off the pity. A man should never show weakness to his enemies. It could make him careless. He watched the horses frolic in the next paddock. McLean kept a remuda of stock horses that he trained himself. They brought top dollar at auction.

The stallion pranced outside and raced along the fence. The remuda joined him from their side—except the remuda stallion, who should have issued a challenge and chased his mares from the fence.

Jackson cursed as he saw the roan stallion limp toward the others. He fetched a lariat from the tack room, then entered the other paddock. It took only a moment to isolate the roan, lasso him, then lead him into the stable.

Once Jackson had the animal in a stall, he examined the favored leg. He cursed again. At that moment, Larry, the foreman's son, came in.

"You," Jackson snapped. "Get in here."

The young man, who was twenty-two, stiffened at the order, but he came forward. Pausing by the stall, he peered cautiously over the planking. "Yeah?"

"The stallion has an injured foot. Why isn't it being taken care of?"

Larry looked blankly at the hoof Jackson held between his legs. The frog was swollen to the point where it extended beyond the horseshoe. "I didn't know—"

"Aren't you supposed to look after the remuda?"

"Yes." Resentment flared in the younger man's eyes.

"Then it's your job to know. The roan is running a fever. He might have gangrene by now. Call the vet—"

"I'll decide when we need the vet," another voice intruded. Hunter walked into the stable, stalked over to the stall and jerked open the door. "I'll check it out."

Jackson dropped the hoof and straightened. He held the furious gaze for a moment, then stepped aside with a shrug. "He's your prize stud. Far be it from me to tell you he's in no shape to cover his mares in his present condition."

He moved outside the stall while McLean took his place. When the rancher pressed on the swollen frog, the stallion nearly leaped the stall, taking the rancher with him.

Jackson allowed himself one tight smile as McLean cursed the proverbial blue streak. The cowboy standing beside him actually trembled. Jackson would have felt sorry for him except for the fact that a fine animal was in pain and might have to be put down because of the young man's lack of care.

The cowboy had a new girl in town and rushed out

every night after the chores to visit her. Jackson had also seen him in town a time or two during the day, hanging out at the restaurant where the girl worked.

"Call the vet," McLean now ordered, his tone quiet but no less deadly. "And then pack up. You'll be riding fences for the next month."

"But I'm the remuda boss," Larry protested.

"Not when you let an animal get in this condition. Get out of here before I take one of the stock whips to you."

The cowboy left after giving Jackson a fulminating glare. Jackson ignored it and turned to McLean. "The broodmares aren't getting enough exercise. They've been cooped up in the paddock for a week. They need to be run."

"I'll handle it," McLean told him.

"When?"

"Now." McLean stepped out of the stall. "Didn't you hear me send Larry out to ride fences?"

"Yeah, but who's going to take care of the horses?"

"I will."

"You're too busy." Jackson studied the roan, who stood quietly, his head drooping. "I'll take over the horses."

"I'm handling the ranch."

"I'll take over the horses," Jackson repeated. He shifted his weight forward, balanced on his toes like a dancer, ready to move if McLean decided to act on the impulse Jackson could see in his eyes.

They'd been sidestepping around each other for three weeks. A head of steam was building between them, ready to erupt like a boiler set on High and then ignored. Jackson felt the swift flow of adrenaline to his muscles. Time slowed to a crawl. He was aware of everything at once—the warm animal scent of the stable, the sense of enclosure coupled with the isolation, the stark need to confront his enemy and slug it out until only one of them remained standing.

The outer door opened. "Larry said we needed the vet. What's wrong?" The foreman let the door bang closed behind him. A swirl of fresh air wafted through the tension.

"Jubal picked up a thorn. He's running a fever," McLean answered, the stiffness going out of his shoulders as he turned to the stall holding the stud.

Russ checked the stallion. "Yeah, this is bad." He glanced up at McLean. "Larry says he's been put on fences for a month."

McLean nodded.

The foreman smiled in stern approval. "Good. Maybe that'll get his mind off that gal in town and back on the business he's supposed to be minding. Who do you want put on the remuda?"

"I'm taking over." Jackson returned McLean's heavy glare with one of his own.

"All right," the foreman said. "I've watched you with your stallion. You know horses."

McLean frowned, but didn't contradict the foreman.

Figuring he'd pressed far enough for one day, Jackson left the stable. That was one up for him.

He saw Dawn checking her fields. The blood rushed hotly through him. She was next.

* * *

"Who is *that?*" Collette demanded. "The guy working with the black horse, is that the brother?"

Dawn glanced up from the soda she was pouring. Hunter was having a summer barbecue. Jackson was in the paddock astride the black stallion, putting the horse through his paces. With his shirt off, his bronze skin gleaming with sweat, he looked the epitome of the American cowboy. Her throat went dry.

She nodded and took a quick sip so she wouldn't have to speak. She didn't like the way Collette was staring at Jackson, as if he were a prime piece of meat and she was in the market for a steak.

Jenny Flynn stared. "He is a hunk."

"If you like 'em wild and fierce," Collette added. She lowered her lashes in a sultry manner. "And I do."

"My cousin works evenings at the motel down at the lake. She said she nearly fainted when he came in and asked for a room. His hair was down on his shoulders and he looked just like a savage," Jenny informed them.

Dawn suppressed her irritation as the two women continued to study Jackson like a prize at a fair.

"Come on. Let's go meet him." Without waiting, Collette strode across the lawn and the road to the paddock.

Jenny hesitated, then followed along after the county beauty queen. Dawn glanced around. Hunter was at the grill. Other couples chatted in groups around the patio. Cola and beer chilled in tubs of ice. Platters of food were spread over three long tables.

All was in order at the cookout. She followed the other two women.

Jackson's stallion was snorting and prancing as she approached the fence where Collette was climbing to the top rail. She thought the animal was showing off at first, until she saw the bared teeth and angry glint in the stallion's eyes.

"Back off," she heard Jackson order Collette, who had perched on the top rail and was swinging one shorts-clad leg as she flirted with him.

"I love a masterful man," Collette said with a laugh and a flirtatious sweep of her lashes, ignoring the command.

Jackson steadied the stallion with a hand on his neck and several soothing words. "This is a young horse. He isn't used to people. Get off the fence," he warned.

"I'm sure you can handle him." Collette flickered her eyelashes at him and swung a leg over the railing.

The stallion snorted, reared, then plunged toward the woman, his teeth aimed for prime flesh.

Jackson cursed and pulled up hard on the reins. Dawn saw the muscles in his arms and chest contract like steel bands as he fought the stallion for control.

"Get down!" Dawn yelled over the squeals of the women and the stomping of hooves as the stallion reared again, his iron-shod feet pawing the air.

Frightened, Jenny backed away from the fence.

Collette clapped her hands. "Ride 'em, cowboy," she encouraged, enthralled by the commotion she was causing. The stallion lunged at her. She flinched, and arms flailing, fell backward off her perch.

Dawn grabbed a handful of pink cotton sweater and tried to steady the other woman. Collette cursed and swung an arm wildly, trying to clutch at something to break her fall. She caught Dawn a glancing blow on her cheek. Dawn held on and managed to keep the other woman from landing on her rear in the gravel.

"He told you to get down. Can't you see you're upsetting the stallion?" Dawn demanded, furiously angry with her friends for their thoughtless ways. "Jackson could have been thrown and hurt."

"*He* could have been hurt?" Collette questioned with an indignant glare. "His horse tried to kill me."

"He did act wild," Jenny chimed in like an echo.

"Because you frightened him."

"That horse ought to be shot," Collette declared, her lips pouty, her eyes flashing now that the danger was over.

Jackson gave her a withering look. "Yeah, and you ought to be horsewhipped. You frightened him with your jumping around and screeching."

"I do not screech—"

The stallion pawed the ground ominously. Jackson looked straight at Dawn. "You may stay. Tell your friends to leave."

His tone was like the sharp end of a lash. She heard collective gasps from the two women. "You'd better go back to the house," she told them.

The horse reared and trumpeted a challenge, then lunged once more at the fence. The women skedaddled.

When they were on the patio and out of hearing, she faced Jackson, her anger over his being in danger mingling with equal anger over his behavior. He swung down from the saddle and headed for the stable. She followed along the fence, then went inside by the outer door while he entered from the paddock.

"Why were you so rude?" she demanded.

"Why were they?"

She gave an impatient exclamation. "They didn't mean to be. They were curious about you and wanted to be friendly. You didn't have to be so mean."

The corners of his mouth indented. She realized he was hiding a smile. She studied him, then the stallion. The animal was happily snuffling around in its oat bucket, not a sign of temperament rippling its ornery hide. Jackson looked pretty complacent, too.

"You did it deliberately," she accused. "You made the horse act up. You wanted to frighten them."

He smiled openly, a cynical gleam in his eye. "It gave them their thrill for the day. After all, I have to live up to my reputation as a wild man."

She crossed her arms over the top of the stall and watched him unsaddle and groom the horse. She decided to take another tack. "I understand why you're defensive, but not everyone is out to get you."

The smile disappeared. "No one will."

The atmosphere in the stable intensified. The air became denser, heavier. "You can't fight everyone all your life," she advised. "If you want to fit in and find a life here, you're going to have to give some...." At his scathing glance, she amended her statement. "Okay, probably the most, until people accept you."

"Accept me? I don't give a damn about whether they accept me or not."

"I think you do." She gave him the same hard scrutiny he turned on others. "You'll have to stop wearing that chip on your shoulder, though. And you'll have to get over what your father did—"

He reached over the planking and caught a handful of her hair. His breath touched her lips as he leaned close. "Don't tell me what to think or feel. Don't interfere in my life. I don't want or need your damn friends."

"Everyone needs someone."

He snorted in contempt and released her. She stayed quiet and simply watched as he groomed his mount.

A sensation akin to pleasure began to grow in her. His hands were skillful as he brushed the silky, rippling hide. One hand rested on the well-muscled frame, the long artistic fingers kneading a tender spot. The horse huffed out a breath and practically sighed in ecstasy.

Dawn found herself sighing, too. She stared in open fascination. Each movement of those wonderfully masculine hands, so strong and capable, yet so subtle in their movements, fired her imagination.

He combed every tangle from the flowing mane and rubbed a dressing into each strand. Her scalp prickled in anticipation as she thought of him doing that for her.

The warmth of the stable closed in on her. She was hot and breathless and sort of shaky. Desire flashed through her like lightning out of a clear sky. She'd never felt anything like it. Longing for his touch grew in her.

After checking the stallion's hooves, he laid his tools aside and turned toward her...and stopped.

His gaze locked with hers.

She didn't know how long they stood there, just looking at each other, silence swirling around them in ominous quiet. A distant storm, invisible but threatening, known only to them, or perhaps only to her, drew closer, as if its intensity matched that inside the stable.

He unlatched the stall gate and stepped outside, only inches from her. The lock clicked shut behind him, its sound unnaturally loud.

Slowly he reached out. "You have a red mark here. Your cheek is swollen." He touched the place.

She flinched slightly. "Collette accidentally hit me when she fell."

"I'll fix it." He crossed the stable to a door at the back. "Come here."

She walked across the hard-pack floor, wariness pulling at every step. Her conscience told her to leave—now.

When he held the door open, she entered the tack room that doubled as an informal office and supply room. He retrieved a medical packet from a drawer, squeezed it to mix the chemicals that would produce an ice pack, then placed it against her cheek himself. He lingered to caress below the ice pack with his thumb.

"You have a wonderful touch," she said, in almost

a whisper. She had seen his anger. She was aware of his strength. Now she learned his gentleness.

Caution nibbled at the fringes of her mind, warning her that she didn't really know this man or the depth of hurt he could inflict on those she loved. And on her.

He moved in close, crowding her.

She felt his warmth before it touched her, then his body was against hers, pressing her against the rough planking of the wall, snatching the breath from her mouth.

"This is what I need, medicine woman," he muttered hoarsely. "The taste of you on my lips. The scent of you in my lungs. The feel of you under my hands."

He kissed her with a harshness that wasn't physical—for all its intensity. She stood frozen under the onslaught, sensing a desperation she didn't want to feel behind the kiss, sensing the need that he would never express—the need for human warmth, for love. She felt a quivering inside as if something might flit away and never be recaptured if she didn't hold on with all her strength.

She steeled herself against the attraction and compelling desire she felt for this man.

Squeezing her eyes shut, she tried to block out the admission while his lips toyed with hers, enticing a response she knew she shouldn't give.

"Kiss me," he said fiercely against her mouth. "Kiss me back the way you do in my dreams."

"No," she said, but it was a denial of herself, not

of him. She wanted his kiss. And she wanted to give back the exquisite torture he practiced on her.

When he sucked at her lower lip, her heart nearly soared out of her chest. When she tried to protest again, he darted inside her mouth, caressing her with velvet strokes of his tongue. He tasted faintly of cinnamon and coffee. With an effort, she turned her head.

He released her mouth, but his arms tightened around her, pulling her closer...closer....

"Kiss me," he demanded and caught her lip between his teeth. She pulled back, but he followed, refusing to let her go.

When she opened her mouth to draw air into her straining lungs, he again took advantage to slip inside and coax a response from her. She shook her head slightly and he moved back.

"Kiss me," he demanded yet again.

"Why are you doing this?" she managed to say.

His mocking smile flashed briefly in the dim stable. "Because. Tell me to stop." It was a challenge.

"The McLeans are my friends."

"This isn't them, it's us—the way you feel, the way I feel, the way it is between us...and has been since that day up on the mountain."

"You're here to hurt them."

"No. Only to claim my own." He spoke in a fierce murmur. "No one will take what is mine away from me. Including you."

She gasped in shock. "I'm not a bone to be won in a tugging match between you and Hunter."

His face softened momentarily. "There isn't a

match. I've seen you kiss him. You don't share *this* with anyone but me. Not with him, only me.''

"But why?" she questioned in a soft cry. "Why? I don't understand.''

"What's to understand?" The smile became sardonic. "Keep this in place." He put the ice pack on her cheek.

She hadn't realized it had slipped off during their kiss. Holding it against the bruise, she considered the situation between her and Jackson, puzzled by the fire and troubled that it didn't exist between her and Hunter, her lifelong friend.

He tilted her chin up so he could look into her eyes. "It's fate. Sometimes it works against you. Sometimes it works for you.''

She shoved his hand away and gave a disdainful sniff. "And it's fated that you and I...that we...''

"Yes." His smile was brief, hard and satisfied, as if he knew something she didn't.

An alarm jangled with muted tones inside her. There was something here that didn't make sense. "You're using me to get at Hunter," she accused, disappointment hitting her like a drenching rain.

He shot her a swift glance of surprise. "Are you denying there's a spark between us? Will you go to *him* and pretend that what you feel is the same as what we share?''

She rubbed the ice pack against her lips, cooling the lingering traces of fire and knowing she wanted to kiss him again, no matter what her conscience said.

Jackson caught her hand and moved the pack to her cheek. "Here's something else you need to think about. You can't make up to him for the loss of your sister.''

She drew back, offended by the notion.

He returned her stare, then bent his head to hers again. Using his thumb, he pulled down her bottom lip, then traced his tongue over it, sending shivers of hot sensation through her. She pressed her lips together.

Ignoring her murmur of protest, he swept his tongue across her lips and teased the corners of her mouth.

"Don't," she ordered sharply.

"Make me," he challenged, his hands going to her shoulders while he avoided her injured cheek by slanting his face to the opposite side.

"I'll make you," a voice said in a low masculine growl behind them.

Hunter stood in the doorway, filling it with the menace of his anger. A couple of ranch hands stood behind him.

Jackson smiled in a way sure to provoke any red-blooded male. "I see you brought reinforcements."

"I don't need help to take care of you. Get away from Dawn. Now."

Jackson shifted, positioning himself in a fighting stance. "Make me," he drawled, letting one hand trail along her cheek to her shoulder.

"Stop it, both of you."

That was all she said. Hunter moved in. Jackson was ready for him. The two men struck out at each other simultaneously, as if the fight were choreographed for a scene in a movie.

Fists landed with solid impact on flesh. With growing horror, she realized they weren't going to feint and parry and do a lot of posturing the way she'd seen boys do a couple of times in high school. This was a no-holds-barred slugfest.

"Stop them," she ordered the cowboys.

"Stay out of it," Hunter countered, stepping back from Jackson's flurry of blows. "Get back to work."

The ranch hands disappeared.

Dawn darted between the two. "I'm not going to let you do this," she said, giving them a stern glare. "This is foolish. You're grown men and know better—"

Hunter took her by the shoulders and pushed her outside the door. He closed it before she could spin around. When she tried the knob, she found it wouldn't turn.

She'd been locked out.

The fight resumed. She heard a low grunt, several curses, then the clatter of tack hitting the floor.

"Hunter, let me in. Right now!"

Only the steady thuds of flesh on flesh answered her. She whirled and ran outside. The cowboys lingered by the ranch truck. "Where's Russ?"

"Over fixing the windmill."

"Open the gate." She leaped into the truck and sped through the opening and across the pasture. She came to a dust-choking halt beside the cattle trough. "We need you at the stable!" she called to him. "Hurry."

He dropped the wrench and climbed in. "What is it?"

"Hunter and Jackson are trying to kill each other. Hunter ordered the hands not to interfere. He locked me out of the tack room."

"What happened to set them off?"

"I—uh— Hunter found Jackson with me."

"Stupid young stallions," Russ muttered. He gave her a glance she didn't miss.

Holding the truck steady over the rough pasture, she protested. "It isn't my fault."

"Well, if it hadn't been you, it would have been something else sooner or later," he admitted. "But it comes down to you."

She pulled through the gate, which the cowboy held for her, and stopped the truck by the stable. She and Russ jumped out and raced inside.

"You boys, come on," he called over his shoulder.

The two men hustled to obey. Dawn tossed them a scornful glare before following at Russ's heels.

The foreman took out his pocketknife, inserted a thin blade into the hole in the lock and had the door open in less than five seconds.

"That's enough," Russ said, stepping across the threshold. "Don't make me have to call the boys in to sort you two polecats out."

Dawn gasped when she entered the small room. Tack coiled in tangles on the floor. Catalogs, papers and pens from the desk lay in scattered piles. But it was the two men who worried her.

Hunter had a cut above his left eye, which was rapidly swelling shut. His bottom lip was cracked and oozing a thin line of blood down his chin. Jackson hadn't fared any better. His jaw sported a blackening bruise. Blood ran from one nostril. Both men could barely stand.

"Well, this is a hell of a note," Russ continued, giving a snort of disgust. "Company up at the main house, and you two amusing yourselves down here like a couple of ten-year-olds."

"Stay out of this, Russ. It has nothing to do with the ranch," Hunter told him.

"I'll call your mother," Dawn threatened. She grabbed chemical ice packs and kneaded them hard. She handed one to Hunter and one to Jackson.

Hunter gave her a fierce glare. "Leave her out of this. It's between him and me, no one else."

"That's an extremely selfish attitude." Dawn gestured to Russ. "Let's leave them alone, then. Let them beat each other to a pulp. They won't kill each other. Their skulls are too thick."

"All bone and no brains," Russ agreed. "Well, get out of my office and into the paddock. Move that black into the cow pasture for now," he ordered one of the ranch hands. "Okay, let's go. You two gonna act like heathens, you gonna do it outside."

Jackson drew himself up, albeit a bit slowly, with grave dignity. "I'm not putting on a show for your friends." He pushed past Russ and Dawn.

Chapter Five

Dawn watched Jackson cross the paddock and head toward his house. Her heart went out to him. A low curse brought her head around. She prepared another ice pack and placed it against Hunter's lip. He held the other to his eye.

"How could you be so stupid?" she demanded.

"Just born that way." He tried to smile, but gave up the effort and slowly started falling. "Turn on the light."

She and Russ grabbed him at the same time.

Their appearance at the patio caused a stir among the guests. Collette rushed forward. "What happened?"

"Just a little tussle," Russ explained in his deadpan way. "Give us some room."

"I can walk," Hunter announced with grave dignity. He did, but only by leaning on his two human supports.

Dawn ignored the burble of questions behind them as they went inside. They guided him to his room without running into Margaret or Anna and laid him on the bed.

"I 'spect I can handle him now," Russ said. "You go take care of his guests. I'll get him cleaned up and tucked in and see that he says his prayers."

Dawn grinned while Hunter managed to snort. A fresh trickle of blood ran from his lip. "Here," she ordered. "Keep these ice packs in place."

She checked on J.J., who looked like a sleeping cherub with his blond curls and long lashes, before returning to the patio and a bevy of eager questions. "He and Jackson had a few words," she said. "Who knows why? You know how men are."

The women laughed while the men pretended to scowl, but many of them were grinning, too. This was another story about the McLean brothers that would be all over the county by morning.

"Okay, who wants to grill the steaks?" she asked.

She got the party organized and back on track. Hunter joined them a half hour later and acted jovial enough, taking the quips of his friends with a good-natured laugh that must have made his lip hurt.

"Sit beside me," he requested when they ate.

She glanced up at the cabin partially hidden in the woods and worried about Jackson.

"Afraid he'll see?" Hunter demanded.

"No. I was wondering how he was. He looked as done in as you did."

"Why don't you go up and check on him?" Hunter asked in a low snarl. "We can get along without you."

Collette listened avidly. The vixen smiled innocently when she saw Dawn looking her way.

Dawn patted Hunter's arm. "Don't be a grouch."

He sat down with a grunt of pain. She took her place next to him and leaned her head against his shoulder for a second in sympathy. She avoided glancing toward the cabin, although she continued to worry about Jackson.

When the guests were gone, she prepared an ice pack and took it to Hunter's room. He was in bed when she knocked, and entered at his okay. She gave him a tablet to ease his pain and placed the pack on his eye. "Keep that there," she scolded, then turned off the light and slipped out.

She played with her nephew for an hour before bathing him and reading a bedtime story. When she went to the kitchen, Anna reported that the two mothers had gone to dinner with friends while she and Hunter were entertaining.

"Why does life have to be so hard?" Dawn asked.

"Because people are an emotional, unpredictable bunch at best."

Dawn sighed and agreed. She looked around the house and patio. "Everything seems to be in order."

"Go on home," Anna said kindly. "I'll stay with J.J. until Margaret gets in. Take one of the ranch trucks. There's no moon to light the way tonight."

Dawn laughed. "I've walked that road so many times I could do it in my sleep."

They said good-night and she left.

At the end of the paddock, she stopped and rested against the rails. The valley was unusually dark, but through the shifting needles of the pine trees, she could see the lights of the cabin.

She wondered how badly Jackson was hurt. She knew Anna would check on Hunter before she went to her own house, but Jackson had no one to tend to him.

Moving on down the barely discernible road, she entered her own empty house, briefly considered going to bed, but went to the kitchen instead. She dumped ice into a small cooler, added some sodas and fruit juice, then packed a bag of first-aid equipment.

Without letting herself think about what, exactly, she was doing, she rummaged through a drawer until she found a flashlight, then headed back up the road. This time she took the path through the woods.

When she stepped on the porch at Jackson's lair, her heart thudded so frantically, she paused to calm herself before knocking on the door.

"It's open," a voice answered from within.

She went inside and set the cooler and package on the table. "Are you in bed?" she called toward the darkened doorway of the bedroom.

"No."

She heard a creaking of springs that gave the lie to his statement. He appeared in the kitchen a second later, his hair disheveled, his eyes bloodshot.

"You look awful. Serves you right," she added.

"Thanks for the sympathy." He managed a grin

although the wince that immediately followed it showed it wasn't without effort.

"I brought you some ice. You need to get it on your nose and jaw. I don't suppose you thought to pick up more chemical packs at the stable."

"I used spring water."

She busied herself adding ice to a plastic bag. "Did you have supper?" She glanced around but saw no signs that he'd eaten anything.

"I don't need a mother," he told her in sarcastic tones.

"Well, you don't need another whomp on the head, either, but I feel like giving you one, you and Hunter both," she added, giving Jackson a stern frown. She saw he'd washed up and put on a clean shirt.

He pulled out a chair and sat down wearily. "Took you long enough to get here. Why did you come?"

"To make sure you were taking care of yourself. I can see you're not."

He snorted. "I've been taking care of myself for longer than you've been wearing bras and panty hose."

She grinned. "That wouldn't be hard to do. I rarely have use of either."

"You will when you nurse a child."

A spasm clutched at her stomach. She gaped at him, unable to think of a reply. A picture of a mother nursing a child leaped into her mind, a dark-haired man seated beside them. She couldn't see the man's face.

Taking herself firmly in hand, she handed him the ice pack and went to the stove. Curiosity ate at her.

"It sounds as if you've had personal experience. Are you married?" It wasn't something she'd even considered.

"No. And haven't been," he said before she could ask. "But I've had friends who were."

She nodded while she opened a can of tomato soup and put it on to heat. She prepared a grilled-cheese sandwich to go with the soup, then set them on the table along with a spoon and a paper towel since she couldn't find napkins in his sparsely stocked pantry.

"Thanks." He took a mouthful of soup and grimaced. "This is barely warm."

"You don't need heat around your face at present," she told him, taking the chair opposite.

He grunted, then reheated the soup while she frowned severely at him.

They were silent while he ate. When he finished, she took his plate and bowl to the sink and washed them.

"You've done your good deed for the day," he told her when she'd finished and turned to assess the damage to his face. "You can go home with a clear conscience."

"My conscience was clear before the fight. It wasn't over me. I was merely the most convenient bone of contention." She stopped, then laughed. "I never realized how apt that cliché was until this moment."

"You laugh and the world smiles," he said, his eyes narrowing as he studied her.

However, he wasn't laughing or even smiling. A

black moodiness had settled over him. He appeared hard and dangerous and angry again.

The laughter died on her lips when she gazed into his eyes. A shudder coursed through her, and she pressed a hand between her breasts to still the racing of her heart.

"How poetical," she murmured, trying and failing to speak in a teasing voice.

He heaved a deep breath and laid a hand over his ribs as if they, too, hurt. "I hate to be a poor host, but I think I'm going to have to go to bed."

When he stumbled slightly upon rising, she looped an arm around his narrow waist, not quite as comfortable doing this for him as she had been for Hunter.

Heat hit her in waves from his lean body. Electric tingles cascaded up and down her arm and side.

Troubled, she admitted none of that had happened when she'd helped Hunter. Her concern had been for her lifelong friend. With Jackson, it was different.

She was aware of every breath she breathed as well as the ones he took. She felt the heat of his skin through his clothing, the weight of his arm when he dropped it across her shoulders.

"You just beg for trouble, you know that?" he grumbled. He let go and sank onto the bed. His hands went to his jeans, then he looked down at his boots.

She tugged on one boot.

"Turn around," he ordered.

She straddled his leg. He braced his other foot on her behind and pushed while she held on to the boot. They got the other one off the same way. While she busied herself pulling the covers back, he shucked his outer clothing.

Clad in a white T-shirt and briefs, he looked every inch a supremely fit male—if she ignored his face.

"Get into bed." She held the covers up.

He did so. "Are you going to join me?"

"Hardly." She put the ice pack on his jaw. "Anything else you need?" She glanced around.

His hand on her arm tugged her to a sitting position beside him. "Kiss me nightie-night," he coaxed.

She hesitated. "Something tells me this isn't a good idea."

"It is." He reached behind her head and urged her to him. Just before their lips met, he murmured, "Why did you go to him first?"

Jackson felt her stiffen and resist his hold on her. He mentally groaned, furious that he'd voiced the question.

God, he was worse than a kid needing attention. He hadn't asked for anything from anyone since he'd come here to beg his father to come home and see his mother before she died. He wouldn't do it again.

"Get out," he muttered, dropping his hand and summoning anger to hide the momentary weakness. "Before I forget my manners. It's been a long time since I've had a woman."

But she stayed beside him, her hip nestled against his. He kept his eyes closed, aware of her scrutiny.

"He couldn't walk. You could."

Her explanation eased a place inside that was tight and achy. He gritted his teeth, wanting her to stay, wanting her to go, wanting her....

It didn't pay to be soft where people were concerned. "Good. I must have hit him harder than he hit me." He would have smiled, but couldn't.

"Hate gets to be a heavy load," she told him, reprimand in her tone. "Hunter's a wonderful person—"

"You're not in love with him."

A heavy silence followed this announcement. He opened his eyes with an effort. His head was pounding. Even his eyelids hurt. Hell, his whole body hurt.

"I won't let you use me to get at him," she finally said. There was regret in the statement, but she didn't deny the accusation, nor his right to make it.

He pushed himself to the limits and reached for her again. Pulling her to him, he tucked her head against his shoulder and inhaled the wonderful spicy scent of her. As bruised as he was—every breath took its toll—he felt his body stir at her nearness.

"Stay," he said. He was too tired to take the word back or even summon anger with himself over the slip.

"I can't."

Not a flat-out "No," but a refusal nonetheless. He heard the censorship of the two mothers behind it—another of the many barriers between them.

Not that it mattered. He wasn't looking for a permanent connection. There was only this…this sexual tension between them, nothing more. He didn't need anything else.

She turned her face away from his. Strands of silken hair fell across him.

He breathed in her freshness and had visions of fields of flowers, of wooded glens and mossy beds.

A soft wind swirled around them. Suddenly he felt as if the whole bed were floating, sailing gently off on a warm, liquid sea of air, guided by a soft glow on the horizon.

In the next instant, they were gone, out of the cabin, away from the ranch and all the strife it entailed.

His mind was playing tricks on him. It had to be.

Before he could convince himself of this, the bed settled gently to the ground of the secluded glen he'd imagined. The scent of mint and water lilies drifted on the air. When he opened his eyes, a hazy green light obscured the tinkling brook he thought he could hear and the balsam pines he could smell.

"Dawn," he muttered, unable to stop the need to say her name, to murmur it in the warm spiciness of her hair.

She stirred in his arms, but didn't move away.

He kissed the strands of silver hair that cascaded over his face. He found the sweet flesh of her nape and sampled it. When he raised his hand, the soreness had disappeared.

He marveled at this.

Holding her hair aside, he brushed kiss after kiss on her neck. He felt her shiver, but she didn't move. Neither did she turn her lips to him. He tugged on her hair.

Slowly, she allowed her head to be turned so she faced him again. He nibbled along the edges of her jaw, then her mouth. It took several minutes before she sighed and tilted her head so he could reach her mouth easily.

Her breath soughed over him, stirring him in places he didn't know could be reached. The world seemed perfect all at once—*this* world, the one that contained only the two of them, no one else.

When her lips moved under his, the rest of the aches in his body drifted away, one by one, until he felt whole and well again in a way he hadn't since he'd been a kid.

She surprised him by taking charge of the kiss, using her tongue to stroke his lips and invade his mouth in sweet forays that had him holding his breath, hoping she would do it again. She did.

When he pushed on her knee, she didn't resist. She lay beside him, her body touching his all the way down his side.

The familiar stirring coursed through him again. The battering he'd taken seemed a long time ago. He wanted her.

Now.

"Stay," he said.

"Sleep," she whispered.

"Your lips are incredibly soft."

"Sleep."

"After we make love."

"Sleep."

She stroked the hair from his forehead. She repositioned the ice pack, then caressed along his neck and chest.

"Sleep."

"All right." He was content to let her take the lead. They had all the time in the world....

* * *

Jackson woke to a pounding headache. He was alone, a blanket tucked around him, a cool bag of water tucked into the groove of his shoulder. He caught a whiff of spicy perfume and lunged from the bed.

Or tried to.

A groan tore out of him, and he sank back down onto the mattress. He was sore right to the bone. A couple of ribs were surely cracked from when he'd slipped and hit the edge of the desk in the tack room during the fight.

He shook his head. That made the pounding worse. He realized that the glen, the sweet haven in her arms—it had all been a dream.

"I was never so humiliated," Margaret informed Hunter, who ate with stoic calm. "Fighting like a bunch of ruffians—and guests right here at the house."

Hunter had already apologized for his lapse in manners and good taste. Dawn knew he wouldn't do so again. She kept her smile under control with an effort. Hunter looked absolutely awful.

The full effects of the bruising had taken a couple of days to show up. Now his face was painted in interesting shades of blue and magenta. He could open his right eye no more than a squint. She figured he deserved the lectures he received from his mother.

"Grown men," Margaret muttered with an indignant huff.

"I know. We should have known better." His sardonic grin cracked his split lip and changed to a grimace.

Dawn wondered how Jackson fared. She hadn't seen him close enough to examine his injuries in the four days since the fight. He'd kept very much to himself.

So had she.

Several times a day, at unexpected moments, she'd relived her lying beside him on his bed, holding him until he'd fallen asleep in her arms. Each time the memory leaped into her consciousness, a spasm of emotion gripped her, clenching her insides into knots.

"Maybe he'll leave soon," her mother suggested.

"No," she said. "The more you fight him, the more determined he'll be to stay."

The two mothers shifted their attention to her.

"You seem to know him well," Margaret said, her mouth tight with disapproval.

It was no secret that she'd been in the tack room with Jackson. She'd admitted he had treated the bruise on her cheek. Naturally Collette and Jenny had spread the word among their friends that Jackson had said *she* could stay but had ordered them to leave. Her mother had reprimanded her several times that week about going into the stable with him.

"Well enough to know he won't budge if pushed." Dawn looked at Margaret, then at her mother, meeting their eyes with a steady gaze. She had nothing to be ashamed of and she refused to be cowed by them.

Hunter, bless his heart, gave her a wink. He and Russ had always been her staunchest supporters when she got into trouble with her folks, usually for traipsing through the woods looking for fairies and following trails to see where they went.

"What does he want here?" Margaret twisted her napkin into a tight spiral.

Dawn imagined the woman would like to do that to Jackson's neck. She sighed. As stubborn as he was, he'd have to be unconscious or dead before he'd give in. He intended to be a thorn in their side until his sense of honor over that long-ago beating was satisfied.

"To find his roots?" Dawn offered. "To claim the heritage that was denied him all his life through no fault of his own?"

"Dawn Alexandra!" her mother exclaimed. She wore the harassed look of a parent with a precocious child.

"He needs to find something of himself," she continued in the assessment of Jackson.

"He needs to leave," Margaret countered. "I've hired another law firm to look into that loan my father made on the ranch. They're estate-and-will specialists. If there's a way to break the will, they'll find it."

"You can't do that," Dawn protested, a fierce need to defend Jackson's interests overriding good sense.

Three pairs of eyes speared her with hostile glances. Anna, entering from the kitchen, cast a searching look her way. Dawn felt the heat seep into her face.

"Whose side are you on?" Hunter asked, wariness leaping into his eyes.

She met his frown with her chin high. "No one's. I just don't see why the sins of the father have to be forced on the child, that's all. Jackson has paid a price all his life. I don't think it's right."

"He's an opportunist," her mother declared. "Who knows if John really was his father—"

"He was," Dawn interrupted. "He most certainly was." Anger swept through her, burning a clean path of righteous indignation through her conscience. She laid her fork on the plate and her napkin beside it. "Would you excuse me?"

"The meal isn't over," Margaret reminded her.

It was a grave social error to leave before a meal was ended. Dawn didn't care. Her appetite had fled.

"I've had enough. Thank you. It was very good." She crossed the patio and hurried toward the road, the need to escape them driving her.

A tall, lean figure stepped out of the shadows of the oak in the front lawn. Jackson grabbed her arm.

"Oh," she said as she was jerked to a halt.

"Don't do that again," he ordered, his jaw clenched so tightly he could hardly speak. His face sported as many interesting shades of blue and green as the other stupid male's she'd just left.

"What?" The word was sharp. She hadn't any idea what he was talking about and she wasn't in the mood to argue with him at the moment.

"Defend me. I can handle my own battles. This isn't a tag-team fight."

"You were eavesdropping." She looked at him as if he were a lower life-form.

"It would have been damned hard not to overhear a shouting match." He gave her arm a shake. "You were the loudest of all. I don't need you to explain me to them."

She jerked her arm from his clasp. "Well, excuse me," she said with an exaggerated drawl. "You're right. You don't need anyone—period." She walked off down the road, leaving him standing there glaring after her. "And neither do I."

His mocking silence followed her all the way home.

Jackson watched the merry scene on the McLean lawn from his position on the new roof over the cabin addition. Dawn lay prone in the grass while her nephew clambered over her, trying to pin her arms down. She roughhoused with the boy. Jackson could hear her laughter and squeals of delight as the kid pretended to bite her neck.

Hunter came out of the hay barn and joined the other two. He stretched out on his side, propped himself up on one elbow, and teased the woman and child by drawing a grass blade under their noses.

Dawn retaliated by tickling Hunter while the now-solemn child looked on. Earlier that afternoon there had been a birthday cake to celebrate J.J.'s third birthday. Dawn had invited Jackson to join them on the patio, but he'd refused.

Jackson winced as he watched the playful group. Longing, old and hurtful from times past when he'd wanted to be the "real" son and live here with the McLean family, hit him with the force of an eighteen-wheeler running straight over his heart.

He finished the last shingle and swung down the

ladder and off the roof. Putting his tools away, he
pictured him and Dawn ending their workday. He saw
them showering together—he now had water in the
cabin—then eating, and still later, enjoying the evening. The night would be all theirs—the solitude, the
breeze, the lull of moonlight.

And each other.

His stomach clenched like a shoe laced too tightly.
Before he could sort through that, he caught a movement at the periphery of his vision. Swinging his head
to the right, he watched Margaret McLean roll past
the stable and down the pasture fence, guiding her
electric wheelchair at a sedate pace along the left edge
of the road.

He'd seen her often of late, out surveying the ranch
like an aging queen checking over her empire, her
eyes, whenever she looked at him, bitter with the
knowledge that she would someday be gone and *he*
would still be here.

He tried to discover within himself if this would
bring him satisfaction, but couldn't. He'd burned with
the pure sweet anger of vindication when he'd arrived
to scout the ranch before making his presence known.
But now... He didn't know what he felt. His gaze
returned to Dawn.

Only where she was concerned were his feelings
simple. He wanted her. The desire was a fierce un-
swerving need that burned brightly, day and night,
sweeping doubt aside as if it were flotsam riding a
wild tide.

As he watched, she gathered her nephew into her
arms and swung him around and around. Her energy

seemed endless. She'd worked with her horses for most of the day.

He wrestled with a need to go over and ask her something in order to hear her voice. He scowled as he recalled asking her to stay with him after the fight. To ensure he didn't do that again, he'd stayed busy, checking the logging operations and working with the horses, getting them into shape for the demands of ranch work.

Fall roundup would bring long days of riding over harsh terrain when they brought the cattle down to the winter pasture and sold off the calves. Life's never-ending cycle.

Pausing on the porch, he gazed again at the wholesome scene. Margaret had joined them and now held her grandson. They were the all-American family of Christmas cards and calendar prints. He was the outsider.

Chapter Six

Dawn surveyed the sky from horizon to horizon. All clear. She hoped it would stay that way for tomorrow's drive to Reno. Nearly everyone was taking off for the weekend to attend the stock show in Reno. Only Anna and Russ were staying behind. They would mind J.J. and keep an eye on both places.

Dawn and the moms were sharing a suite at one of the big hotels. Hunter had a room across the hall and had already booked a dinner and show for them. The ranch hands would be off, too. It would be three days of fun for all.

No one had said whether Jackson was going, and she hadn't asked. Since her outburst at lunch that day, she was keeping a low profile.

She gave the sky one more sweep. The crops should be okay for three days. Last year a hailstorm had wiped out most of the echinacea and valerian before the final harvest.

There were four horses in training and another eleven being boarded. She'd put her charges through their paces yesterday afternoon. All was in order. She hoped. It was impossible to account for everything in life.

She turned from her contemplation of the sky and looked toward the cabin on the rise beyond the stable. *He* was one of the most unpredictable elements she had ever known.

Sometimes she caught him watching her, his expression closed and moody. When he drove in or out on the ranch road, he nodded to her, but didn't stop. And yet, his eyes always sought her out anytime they were in sight of each other. She looked for him, too.

Sometimes their eyes met, and she felt she was being consumed by him. But he never approached her.

She sighed and continued her early-morning walk along the paddocks. The satisfaction of watching her plans and efforts come to fruition was still there, but the peace she used to find on her early-morning jaunts was missing.

At that moment, the cause of her unrest emerged from the woods and came toward her. Her heart thudded painfully.

He was powerfully attractive. His stride was long, and he looked as rangy as a timber wolf. Like the wolf, there was self-possession in his carriage, pride in the tilt of his head, and an unflinching directness in the way he faced the world.

She also thought he was a man of courage. He had the sharply honed integrity of one who was innately honest but had learned to be cautious of mankind. He looked wonderfully fit and healthy in his jeans, chambray shirt and boots.

During the past two weeks, even over the Fourth of July, there had been a flurry of activity at the cabin. Delivery trucks had come and gone. Workmen had been in and out, too. The mothers had talked incessantly about Jackson and what he could possibly be doing up there.

Dawn looked at his lips and imagined his kiss. She gazed at his hands and imagined his touch. Turning from his disturbing scrutiny, she gathered her poise and ignored the wayward desires that coursed through her.

"Good morning," he murmured, stopping near her. His voice was deep and darkly sensual, stroking across her nerves like the vibrant caress of a violin bow. "It's a fine day, isn't it?"

"So far." She gave him a wary glance. His bruises were gone, and he looked as handsome as ever, and as tempting. Her pulse pounded heavily through her veins, making her as aware of her own body as she was of his.

His sigh was dramatic. "You've implied I lack the common amenities. Yet, when I try to show you I can be as civilized as the next person, you view me with suspicion."

"One should be wary when a wolf is friendly," she said.

He laughed. It was as intriguing as the chant that

had first drawn her to him. She smiled, knowing she shouldn't encourage him but unable to refrain.

Swinging into step beside her, he continued his teasing. "I've had a good week, thank you. The work on the cabin is coming along nicely." He paused. "Would you like to see it?"

She gazed into his eyes and for a second saw beyond the sardonic humor to the very heart of the man. She saw his loneliness and his fear of trusting another human. She blinked and the moment was gone. Again his eyes were darkly opaque, his thoughts mysterious.

"Yes," she said. "I'd like to see it."

Linking her hand in the crook of his arm, he escorted her across the road and into the woods. When the path narrowed, he took her hand and led the way. At the cabin, he opened the door and let her enter first.

She gasped in surprise, causing him to laugh again.

In place of the crude shelves that had once lined the wall, built-in cabinets of limed oak occupied two sides of the room. Butcher-block counters complemented the cabinets. The gas stove fit neatly into a space made for it. A new sink and refrigerator plus no-wax vinyl squares on the floor had turned the old room into a modern kitchen. The fourteen-inch-square logs had been cleaned, sealed and chinked with white caulking.

"Right out of a magazine ad," she complimented, finishing her perusal. "I like it that you preserved the flavor of the log cabin along with the modern conveniences. When did you do all this?"

"I ordered the cabinets when I first moved in. They

arrived last week, along with the refrigerator and sink. I hired some men to help me install them.''

''It's beautiful.'' She looked toward the closed doors at the rear and side. ''What else have you done?''

He let her explore the other room, the one that used to be the bedroom. It was now a master bathroom, complete with tub and shower, double sinks with a mirror and makeup lights over the counter and a private alcove for the toilet. A laundry room, ready for a washer and dryer and a utility sink, drew an exclamation of delight from her.

''But where do you sleep?''

''Under the stars. My bedroll is out back.''

She absorbed this information in a remote part of her mind while images of snuggling down in a sleeping bag with him filled her conscious thoughts.

''What are you thinking?'' He was suddenly close to her.

She shook her head, trying to dislodge the visions that fractured her composure. ''Nothing. What's in here?''

Rushing from the temptation to touch him, she opened the other door and stepped into the new wing. ''It's big,'' she said, confused by the size of the addition.

The scent of sawdust tickled her nose. Curls of planed wood littered the floor where doors had been fitted. Walls were defined by two-by-fours. Pipes and plumbing fixtures were in place.

''I was only going to add a couple of rooms, but

it doesn't cost much more to put in extra bedrooms and baths.''

"How many?'' She crossed the subflooring and counted the rooms off the long hallway. ''Four bedrooms?''

He nodded and gestured toward one large, framed area. ''This will be the master bedroom. The last bedroom is a suite with its own bath and sitting area. My aunt Maggie might decide to visit someday.''

She was immediately intrigued by his family. ''Do you have other aunts or uncles?''

"Yes. My grandfather had six brothers. Three of them are living. I have one uncle in addition to Aunt Maggie. On my mother's side,'' he added. ''I don't know anyone from the distaff side of the family.''

"Your father had a brother. He died a couple of years ago. There are two sisters, one in California, the other in New York. They rarely visit.''

Jackson's eyebrows lifted slightly as if skeptical about this news but he said nothing.

"The first McLean to settle here was a Civil War veteran,'' she continued. ''He returned home to Kentucky to find his wife and three children had died of a fever while he was gone. He sold out and headed west.''

"He apparently found someone else to share his bed.''

"Yes. He married a girl who had run away from her father and the man her father had betrothed her to. John Allen McLean hid her in his cabin and held off her father and suitor—until it became necessary to get a preacher in to marry them. She was expecting your great-grandfather by then.''

''It must have been a real hardship to get her pregnant so she wouldn't have to marry the other man.''

''Don't be such a skeptic. The story is considered very romantic in these parts. The Historical Society ladies loved it.''

He gave a soft snort, but there was amusement in his eyes. ''More than one man has played the fool for a woman. John Allen McLean probably wasn't the first or the last McLean to do so.''

''Would you?''

He rubbed a finger along his jaw. ''I did, didn't I?''

His eyes darkened. He moved the two steps that brought him within touching distance of her.

''What do you mean?'' She tried to look only mildly interested, but she was curious about him and the other women who had been part of his life.

''You, me and McLean that day in the stable.''

''That wasn't about me. That was a fight that had been waiting to happen for eleven years.''

He touched her hair, running a hand down the length of it, then clasping a handful and watching it cascade through his fingers. ''It was you. He knows I want you...and that I'll fight for you.''

For a second she was stunned. ''That's nonsense,'' she stated firmly when she recovered. But her heart trembled.

''Okay,'' he conceded. ''He knows I won't back away from a fight if he offers one. But the rest is true.''

She searched his eyes, but there wasn't a trace of laughter in them. She tried to find meaning in those cool, dark depths, but he hid his emotions too well.

He touched her cheek, then her mouth with the tips of his fingers. Hot-and-cold shivers ran along her nerves.

"I shouldn't tell you that," he continued softly, but with such sardonic overtones, she realized he was merely taunting her. "A woman has all the advantages already. A man shouldn't give her more."

"Ha." She batted his hand aside and returned to the kitchen, away from the intimacy of the unfinished bedroom.

"Breakfast?" he offered, following.

Knowing she should leave him to his own cynical company, instead she nodded. He held a chair for her at the table, then served her a cup of coffee. After freshening his cup, he cooked bacon and scrambled eggs for them. While the eggs finished, he set out two mismatched plates, each chipped on the edge. She recognized them as those she used to play with years ago in this same cabin.

"Sorry about the dishes. That's something the woman usually picks out. Maybe you could help me."

She considered selecting household furnishings with him. A longing rose in her. She contemplated life with this man in this house. It could be heaven. Or hell.

"Your wife will want to do it."

He laughed again, but it wasn't playful this time. "No wife. Never has been, never will be."

The hurt struck suddenly, like an unseen arrow shot from the forest straight to her heart. "Never?" She couldn't keep the question from coming out dead serious.

He set the meal on the table, then stopped and studied her. His facial muscles seemed to shift and set harder under his tanned skin. "Never."

She wanted to leave, but pride wouldn't allow it. "What if you fall in love?" she challenged instead.

"Like my old man did with my mother? Leaving her with a kid and a heart full of dreams?" He shook his head, took the chair opposite her and picked up his fork.

"Not like that. A real marriage."

"'Till death us do part'?"

"Yes."

"Don't set your hopes on that one. Nothing lasts that long, especially between a man and woman."

"My parents' marriage did. That's one reason my mother worries about me being with you. She thinks you'll break my heart. Will you?"

His gaze was stern and unbending. "That only happens if you fall in love. Don't."

The one word, spoken harshly, was a warning— one she knew she should heed...and one she was afraid she couldn't.

She decided a new topic was called for. She couldn't match his hard-edged view of life and love with any logic that would change his mind.

"Are you going to get a new table and chairs? These rickety old things are a bit out of place, unless you're going to decorate in early cowboy-line shack style.''

His smile flashed again. For the rest of the meal, they talked about how he would finish the cabin, and some color schemes that would go well in it.

''You can't call a four-bedroom house a cabin, though,'' she mused over a fresh cup of coffee. She rose and followed him to the front porch when he stood and held the door open. They sat side by side and watched the sun rise.

''I guess not,'' he agreed.

''It's a house built for a family.''

''No.''

''Yes,'' she insisted. He might fool himself, but he couldn't fool her. He was preparing a home for his family, whether he admitted it or not. ''Then why do it?''

He gave her an irritated stare. ''That's the way a woman's mind runs. House, ergo home. Home, ergo kids. It doesn't always have to follow that route. Maybe I intend to have a woman here on an occasional visit.''

''Like your aunt Maggie?''

A slow grin bloomed on his lips. ''Yeah, like Maggie. Or you. I think I'm ready for dessert,'' he murmured on a deepened note. ''I think you're going to be it unless you leave right now.''

His gaze at her mouth held her spellbound until finally she had to close her eyes or look away. She chose to close her eyes. His breath fanned her lips for a second before he touched her mouth with his.

Flares went off inside her, lighting up her world

brighter than any sun ever could. This time she didn't try to think or protest the sensations that ran riot through her blood. She set the cup aside, then lifted both hands to encircle his neck. She pushed her fingers into the thick black hair and pulled him closer.

When his tongue stroked her lips, she opened to him. In a moment, it wasn't enough. They twisted toward each other, trying to touch everywhere at once. Finally he lifted her and placed her across his lap. Then they meshed together perfectly.

She trembled with the emotions that ran through her and sometime between the first breath of that kiss and the last one, when he tore his lips from hers and buried his face in her hair, she acknowledged that she might, she just might, be falling in love.

"Dawn," he said. He kissed her neck, then behind her ear. "The beginning of light."

He lifted his head and gazed into her eyes. For a second, before passion burned out all else, she saw wariness and perhaps bafflement. Then he came to her again, and nothing else mattered.

He moved his hands restlessly over her back as the kiss deepened, then slipped them under the shirt she wore. Cradling her on one arm, he slid his other hand over her back and along her ribs, exploring until finally he brushed the underside of her breast. His chest lifted in a sharply indrawn breath.

They gazed at each other endlessly. She didn't protest his intimate touch. A sense of togetherness washed over her. Everything felt right.

Gently he cupped her breast and then held her for a long time. He kissed her—many short but tender kisses. Then he simply held her and stared into the distance where the sun picked out the highest peaks with warm streamers of light. He began to stroke the tip of her breast, causing it to bead tightly, sending spirals of electricity to lodge deep within her.

"When I get the house built, will you come live with me?" he asked, driving the breath from her body.

No answer came to mind, only a heightened elation coupled with a sense of pending disappointment.

He smiled into her shocked eyes. "The mothers have raised you well. Are you offended that I would ask without offering the ring you've been led to expect with it?"

"I don't know. I'm too stunned to think right now." She stilled his hand on her breast. "Why do you want me to live with you?"

"You're a beautiful woman. You respond to me the same way I respond to you. I want you in my bed."

The simple sweetness of being together and watching the sunrise faded as he put their relationship on a strictly physical plane.

"An affair doesn't require that we occupy the same house," she told him.

He cupped her face and kissed her again, on and on, until they were breathless and her heart pounded so hard against her ribs she thought the bones would crack with the beauty and urgency of it.

When he released her, he pressed his forehead to hers and murmured softly, "Does McLean make you feel this way? Do you react to him as you do to me?"

Birdsong and crickets chirped around them, but she heard only a fragile sound, like crystal breaking. She pushed against his chest, separating them, and struggled out of his arms to stand on the porch.

"Is that what this is all about? Getting one up on Hunter? Humiliating him by getting me to move in?"

He rose and stood beside her, his eyes watchful, wary. "You tell me. Why do you let me kiss you and touch you like there's no tomorrow if you're not interested?"

"I thought we were falling in love." She met his gaze levelly, refusing to be ashamed of her feelings.

He scoffed. "Words are cheap, but I can promise you this—as long as we're together I'll be true to you. There will never come a day when you'll wonder where I am or what I'm doing. I'll make sure you know."

She viewed the words from every angle. A declaration of love it wasn't, but... "That sounds a lot like a commitment," she said, challenging him to deny it.

"For as long as it lasts."

"How long will that be?"

"I don't know." He was brutally honest.

"Have you had other arrangements like this?"

"No." He smiled, a sardonic gleam in his eye. "You're the first. If you drive me crazy with questions, you may be the last."

"What if we have children?"

The smile disappeared. "No kids. That's not part of the deal."

"No future. No promises. Just sex. Is that the offer?'' she finally asked. She managed to keep her tone cool and disinterested.

It wasn't a cold-blooded offer—not when his heart had knocked against her breasts the way hers was doing against her ribs; not with the desire still evident in the hard ridge behind his jeans. However, she had to face the truth. ''I think this is part of your revenge tactics against the McLeans. I won't be used that way.''

He gave her a thoughtful perusal. ''McLean and I would probably fight about you being here,'' he admitted. ''Does it matter?''

He sounded as if he'd asked merely to be polite. He wasn't worried about the outcome.

''Yes. Because whatever happens between us could hurt someone else,'' she declared.

''And your loyalty is to him.''

She stepped to the ground and away from the hands that had stroked her so sweetly she wanted to melt into his caresses and say yes without a backward glance.

''My loyalty is to those I love and who love me.'' She tried to match his matter-of-fact tone. ''I'd have to be crazy to even consider such a lukewarm suggestion.''

He bounded off the porch and caught her to his lean, masculine length. ''Lukewarm? I'll show you lukewarm,'' he threatened. ''Then I'll show you *hot*.''

He kissed her again and stroked her body with subtle movements of his own. When he pressed one hard thigh between hers, she nearly melted. He was holding most of her weight now, but it didn't seem to bother him. He kissed her for a long moment, then set her away. His breath was labored.

"How long do you think we can withstand the need for each other?" he asked in a thickened voice.

She said the first thing that came to mind. "I don't know. But I won't hurt others—"

"All right." He let her go. "You're free. Fly away, ladybug. But know this—the next time you kiss McLean, you'll think of me."

She shot him an affronted glare. Head high, she sailed across the grass until she reached the safety of the woods; then she fled down the path to the shelter of a greenhouse, there to get herself under control before facing her mother for the day. She would never go near that...that savage again.

Jackson watched until she disappeared into the woods, then reappeared on the road. He saw her enter a greenhouse to work among her plants. He had work to do, too.

Licking his lips, he found the taste of her lingered like chocolate after the last bite was gone. Desire splintered like a shattered sun inside him. There was danger here that he couldn't quite grasp.

Being around her, he kept getting befuddled. He'd thought to stay here only long enough to show McLean and his mother that he couldn't be run off. He hadn't meant to build a damn big house as if he were going to homestead here permanently.

He'd recognized the spark between him and Dawn from the first. He'd meant to use the attraction as just another thorn in McLean's hide. He *hadn't* meant to let it get the better of his survival instincts.

Or to invite her to share his home. He didn't know what hole that lamebrain idea had sprung from, but he had a strong feeling he'd better watch himself.

By damn, the woman was a witch. He'd all but fallen on his knees in front of her.

Disgusted by his unpredictable actions, he forced his mind to the never-ending chores of ranch life. Gathering tools from the barn, he went to repair a section of fence he'd noticed was leaning.

Blasted animals. They were forever poking their heads through the barbed wire—the barbs didn't bother them at all—and sampling the grass on the other side. He glanced back at the Ericson property in time to see Dawn emerge from the greenhouse and head for her home.

His heart played leapfrog in his chest. He cursed loudly and roundly. It didn't help. He leaped into his truck and took off for the pasture as if a mad bull were on his tail.

He worked steadily until noon. The mares had all come over to check him out. They'd hung around for half an hour in case he decided to feed them some oats. When he didn't, they went back to grazing the lush summer grass.

When the sun was past noon, he tossed the tools in the back of the truck and headed to the bunkhouse where Anna would have a hearty lunch ready for the hands. For supper, the cowboys heated leftovers in a microwave oven.

The modern-day ranch, he scoffed, remembering the summer hogan he and his grandfather had shared and the clay oven where they'd baked their flat rounds of bread. In the winter, they'd moved back into the tiny house with his mother. Later his aunt had moved in and taken care of them.

After closing the last gate behind him, he eased onto the gravel ranch road, then stopped. McLean's mother was at the side of the road in her wheelchair. She was turning its wheels by hand. Her face was flushed, and she had worked up a sweat. He leaned out the window.

"Something wrong?"

She gave him a cold stare. "Of course, something is wrong. The battery quit on my chair. Would you please have Hunter come out here."

Jackson ignored the imperious order. "I'll give you a lift back to the house." He opened the passenger door, then climbed down. He wheeled her to the side of the truck.

"This isn't necessary. Hunter can—"

"Ma'am, you're almost a mile from the ranch quarters. I don't have a notion where McLean is. I'm your best bet for getting back anytime soon." He bent down. "Put your arm around my neck."

He had to give her credit, she didn't shriek like most women would have when he hoisted her into his arms, then onto the passenger seat of the truck. He slammed the door, placed the wheelchair in the back and climbed in.

They arrived at the house in frigid silence. Anna came out on the patio when she saw him lift Margaret out of the truck and into the wheelchair. He pushed her up the walk.

"What happened? Are you hurt?" she asked her friend.

"Of course I'm not hurt. The wheelchair quit."

This was said in such disgust, as if the wheelchair had thwarted her on purpose, that Jackson had to smile. Anna saw it and smiled back.

"Come inside. I've brought lunch up. Hunter has already eaten. He and Russ are checking a carcass in one of the sections. It looks as if a cougar has decided to move in and live off the fat of the land." She glanced at Jackson. "Why don't you join us? The hands have already eaten, and the bunkhouse kitchen is cleared up."

He saw Margaret stiffen, but she said nothing.

"Thanks, but I'll find something at my place." He headed for the truck, then stopped. "You should get a cell phone if you're going to wander around by yourself out here."

"We used to have a ranch dog who stayed with her," Anna said, when Margaret didn't answer. "Calhoun was seventeen when he died."

Jackson nodded and left. He thought of the mutt he'd grown up with. He'd loved that old dog, told it all his secrets. When it died, he hadn't replaced it.

He thought of solemn little J.J. who never spoke. Maybe the boy just needed someone special to talk to.

Chapter Seven

Friday afternoon, Jackson watched McLean load his mother into a big ranch wagon and stop for Dawn and Mrs. Ericson at their house. They were heading for the stock show in Reno. He decided a visit to the city was in order.

He tossed some clothes into a bag, zipped it and was on his way in another fifteen minutes. He drove seventy when he hit the four-lane highway until he spotted the ranch wagon ahead of him. He followed, keeping a car or two between them like a detective in a grade-B movie.

Entering Reno, he stayed with them until he saw McLean stop at one of the big casino hotels and get out. When he was sure they were staying there, he parked, waited twenty minutes, then went inside with his bag.

"Sorry, we're full this weekend," the desk clerk said, not looking the least bit regretful.

Jackson hesitated, then assumed a puzzled expression. "How about under McLean? My brother was supposed to book the rooms."

The clerk perked up. "McLean? Ah, Mr. McLean and his party have already checked in. Are you staying with him?"

"No, I wanted a room of my own."

"Just a minute, please." The clerk disappeared into the manager's office.

Jackson felt guilty for all of thirty seconds, then he shrugged. Hotels kept a few rooms available for important guests who dropped in. It was time he got some use from the McLean name. It was, after all, the one that was on his birth certificate.

The clerk returned, smiling broadly. "We've had a cancellation," he said. "The manager okayed letting you have the room. Actually, it's an upgrade to a suite."

Jackson knew when to be grateful. "Hey, that's great. Thanks for checking it for me."

He signed in, declined the use of a bellhop and headed for the elevators. His room was on the concierge level. He showered and changed, then went to the casino. Choosing a slot machine where he could see the elevators, he dropped in five quarters and hit the button to spin the cylinders.

A tall blonde stepped out of the elevators. His heart thumped painfully, then settled down. The woman's eyes met his. She gave him a flirty glance from under her lashes.

He pretended not to notice. He dropped another five quarters in the one-armed bandit and got ten back. He parlayed the ten into twenty, then sixty, then a hundred. An hour later, he dropped the last five into the slot. He got ten back. So he ended the same as he began.

He smiled at the irony. There was a lesson to be learned here if he only knew what it was. He wandered around the casino, noted there was a dinner and show that night and wondered if Dawn and her companions would be attending. A line had formed for the first performance. He bought a ticket.

He was seated at a table for six, the last one in the row. It gave him a clear view of the door. His hunch paid off. Dawn arrived with her group shortly before dinner was served. The manager seated them at a table in front, one prepared to accommodate Mrs. Mc-Lean's wheelchair.

Jackson watched with cynical amusement as the waiter hovered over them. McLean ordered champagne for the ladies, a Scotch for himself. Both arrived almost before the words were out of his mouth.

Finally Jackson let himself look at Dawn. Her hair was done up on top of her head in a casual style that looked as if it might tumble down at any moment. Silvery strands wafted around her face and neck, inviting a man to nuzzle them aside and kiss her wherever they brushed her pale skin.

She wore a long pleated skirt of pale blue. Her silk shirt of blue-and-lavender print was open down the front, revealing a blue shell underneath. A single strand of pearls adorned her neck. Pearl studs gleamed demurely at her ears.

Her flawless complexion was enhanced with a hint of color across her cheeks, and she had darkened her eyebrows and lashes. She was lovely and ethereal and seemed as far from his sphere as a distant star. Her refusal to share his home still smarted. He'd never asked a woman to do that. If he were wise, he wouldn't do it again.

Watching her, he realized she belonged in this sophisticated environment, laughing and chatting with the McLeans, waving to someone she recognized—a recently-elected state senator, who then stopped by their table.

Jackson watched while Dawn introduced him to the mothers and to McLean. The man lingered, smiling and talking, his eyes on Dawn most of the time. Yeah, with her for a wife, the man would probably make it to the White House. She was gracious and at ease and so beautiful it hurt to look at her. Why would a woman like that want to live in a remodeled log hut with a bastard half-breed?

"Good evening," a woman said, taking one of the empty chairs. The table filled up with two couples and their grandmother who was treating them to a night out, the older woman explained. Jackson exchanged first names with them and managed a bland conversation while they ate.

"Excuse me," he murmured after the meal, seeing Dawn rise and leave her group. He followed her out of the theater. She went to the elevator. He hurried after her, calling himself all kinds of a fool, but there was something he had to know, and he could only learn it from her.

The eyes were the most revealing part of human expression. He would know when she looked at him whether she was embarrassed to be seen with him. He stepped into the elevator just as the doors swished closed behind him.

She glanced his way. Her eyes opened wide, then sparkled like a magic fountain as she smiled. He saw surprise, then warmth. No subterfuge. No coy pretense. She smiled, puzzled, a bit wary, but friendly.

Something in him that had jeered at his need to test her like this, quieted and slunk off into the darkness of his soul. He experienced a strong contraction in his chest and couldn't tell what it was, only that it was painful and somehow sweet at the same time.

"Jackson!" she exclaimed. "I didn't know you were coming down. You should have said something."

"It was an impulse." He wasn't going to admit he'd followed her, that he'd wanted to observe her with friends and see how she acted with them and if she was different when she was with him. It was something he had to know.

She laughed, and he wanted to kiss her so badly, he would have if the elevator hadn't stopped and another couple hurried in, making him feel crowded in the small car.

He and Dawn were silent the rest of the way. He stepped out with her at her floor.

She retrieved a key from her evening bag. "Mar-

garet is developing a headache,'' she explained. ''I've
come for her pills in case it's a migraine.''

Jackson opened the door for her, then waited in the
parlor while she went into a bedroom. She returned
in less than a minute. ''I have to get back to the show.
The others will be expecting me.''

''I know. I saw you.''

''You were there?'' She gave him an odd glance
as they returned to the elevators. ''Why didn't you
come over and say hello?'' The question was a challenge—one he didn't quite understand. There were
other meanings layered in it.

''Because.'' He punched the Down button. ''Don't
worry. I won't start a fight.'' He gave her a cynical
smile. ''No one will know you were with the bastard
brother rather than the legitimate one.''

She was silent for a moment. ''You think I'm
ashamed to be seen with you,'' she finally said before
they stepped into the busy lobby. Her lips thinned,
and he realized she was angry. Really angry.

He shrugged. Her hand on his arm stopped him
when he would have left her there. He glanced at her
hand and noted the paleness of her skin beside his.

''Night and day,'' he murmured, pointing to their
images in the mirrors along the wall. ''The two can
never mix. You look like an angel who checked your
wings at the door. I'm the lord of darkness.'' He
smiled at the comparison even as he admitted it was
true.

She shook her head. ''That isn't the way I see us.
I see a man and a woman, each the complement of
the other.''

Slowly, deliberately, she stroked his jaw, then cupped his face in her hand. Stretching up, she kissed him on the mouth, there in a roomful of people, in plain sight of anyone who cared to look.

She didn't close her eyes, but stared into his the whole time. Then she stepped back and waited for his reaction. There was something of a challenge in the pale blue depths, as if she dared him to...to do what?

Caution learned the hard way kept him from enclosing her in his arms and kissing her until all thoughts of tomorrow melted from him.

"You'd better rejoin your party before your mother sends out the watchdog," he advised.

She pushed a strand of hair off her temple, her anger still evident. "You're right." When he didn't move, she stuck her nose in the air and stepped inside the theater.

Jackson watched the sway of her slender body as she walked off. Somehow she'd turned the tables on him. He'd wanted to confront her and assess her reaction. He'd expected— He didn't know what he'd expected—that she would ignore him, pretend not to know him or act cool and indifferent toward him.

She'd done none of those.

He recalled the way her eyes had lit up upon seeing him. He touched his mouth. She'd kissed him in public. He stepped into the empty elevator and beat a trail to his room, two floors above hers. There were things he needed to sort out before he saw her again.

Dawn waved goodbye to Hunter, who had a meeting with the other officers of the local Cattlemen's

Association. He went into a restaurant while she continued her exploration of the livestock show and auction.

She ambled past pens of prime beef representing eighteen types developed over centuries of breeding. Lean was the in thing now, and ranchers were adding new hybrids to old varieties in an attempt to keep pace with the tastes of the buying public. Even oxen and buffalo were available for stud service.

A shadow fell across her as she stopped to scratch the fuzzy ears of a Hereford that had stuck his head over the fence and given her a soulful stare.

"Hi. Would you look at this spoiled baby?" she said, then smiled up at Jackson, knowing it was him by the way the air went all hot and tingly with electricity.

"All males love to be petted."

"But women have to be careful. Sometimes you bite."

Green flashes of fox fire sparkled in his eyes. "Never with you," he vowed.

She breathed in the hot July air. The scent of popcorn, corn dogs, caramel apples and lemonade mingled with that of the hundreds of animals brought to the show by proud owners. The auction would begin at one that afternoon.

Jackson fell into step beside her. "Where's the watchdog?"

She let her annoyance show. "If you mean Hunter, he's at a meeting. If you mean my mom, she's gone shopping with Margaret."

"So you're on your own."

"Until the auction begins. I'm to save Hunter a seat."

"You looking for anything special?"

"No. I'm here to enjoy the outing, not to buy."

"I notice you don't have a riding horse."

She laughed. "I train horses for six hours a day for a living. After that, I usually prefer to walk."

"Especially in the woods."

His insight surprised her. "Yes, I like the quiet of the woods and the sense of having the world to myself. Oh, look." She touched his arm and pointed.

A silvery gray mare with a white mane and tail, the faint shadows of dappling across her back, reached over a stall and neatly slid the latch open. With a nudge of her nose, she pushed the door open and took two steps outside.

"Quiet," Jackson ordered softly. "She's ready to bolt." He moved forward, as silent as a cat.

Dawn stayed where she was.

The mare eyed Jackson and tossed her head. Her mane waved gracefully in the breeze like banners lofted in the name of freedom. Jackson spoke in a soft, chanting singsong to the animal. His movements were slow and controlled.

Dawn smiled and waited, knowing the outcome before it happened. Just before Jackson reached the animal, a shout echoed along the narrow walkway between the stables and the pens.

A man rushed at the mare, causing her to rear and snort in anger. Her ears went flat, and she lunged at Jackson with her teeth bared. Dawn pressed her hands together between her breasts. She didn't move or cry out.

Jackson avoided the mare's teeth and caught a handful of mane with one hand and the nostril groove with the other. Using his weight, he pulled the mare's head down and backed her into the stall.

"Here, stand back!" the man ordered. "I'll get her in." He swung a heavy crop at the mare, hitting her above the eyes. The mare screamed in pain and anger.

Jackson ducked the thrashing hooves and slammed the stall door. He caught the man's wrist before another blow fell. Dawn breathed a sigh of relief.

"Hey, watch it." The man tried to wrench his arm from Jackson's grasp.

"Leave the mare alone," Jackson ordered.

"She's my horse. I'll do what I damn well please. I'm going to teach her a lesson she won't forget—"

"Hit her again, and I'll take that crop to you."

Dawn waited while the two men eyed each other. Finally the mare's owner backed down.

"You interested in her?" he asked craftily. He glanced at Dawn, then back at Jackson. "She'll make your lady a fine riding horse."

Jackson snorted and resettled his Stetson. "Not likely. A man would have to work a long time to get rid of the bad habits and overcome the poor training this horse has received. It would take a year before she'd be fit to ride—if she isn't ruined to the bit already."

The owner flushed rust red and looked ready to explode. Jackson didn't notice. He dusted himself off and ambled back to Dawn. "Let's get out of here before I call the stable manager,'' he said loudly enough to be heard.

Dawn took his arm and let him lead her away from the area. She looked back with regret at the beautiful mare.

"She'll be okay," Jackson assured. "He won't beat her while there are others around to keep a watch on him."

"But what about when he gets her home?"

"She's for sale. He can't handle her. He's anxious to sell her to some other chump that falls for her color and conformation." He gave Dawn a sideways glance that took in her jeans and T-shirt, appreciation in his gaze. "You could get a good price for her."

A blush of pleasure warmed her face. "I can't afford a horse. She may not be a good saddle horse, but she's still worth a few thousand."

He shrugged and dropped the subject. Dawn considered her finances, but couldn't justify the expense. Maybe someone would buy the mare and give her a good home as breeding stock. Maybe Hunter would be interested.

Jackson gave her a speculative glance. "Come on, I'll buy you a corn dog."

"Wow. The last of the big spenders."

He clasped her neck. "Don't get smart. I'll withdraw the offer."

Dawn laughed. She put aside the memory that this was the man who had offered her a place in his home as a bed partner, who wanted her on a temporary basis. For the next two hours, she forgot the problems and had fun. They strolled along the pens, eating and talking about the animals on display.

"Oh, my gosh, the auction!" she exclaimed, glancing at her watch. She was five minutes late. "I was supposed to get there early and save Hunter a seat."

Jackson went with her as far as the door. There he left her with a tip of his hat and a wave. She gave her ticket to the woman and rushed inside. Ten minutes later, Hunter found her and settled beside her on the hard wooden bench.

"I've found a bull I like." He pulled out the stock program. "It will be a couple of hours yet. They're doing the stock horses first."

Dawn observed the first five group sales with interest, but she saw nothing to get excited about. The sixth horse set her heart to pounding. It was the dappled gray.

The mare stepped into the ring with her head high and glanced around with a disdainful snort. She lifted her feet, prancing with the dainty grace of a ballet dancer.

"Oh," Dawn breathed, spellbound. She did a quick mental calculation; there was no way she could juggle her finances to include a horse she didn't need. She sighed and glanced around the crowd, wondering who would get the mare and if they would know how to train the animal.

She thought of hands that could stroke and soothe or caress and excite, hands that were sure in their touch, hands that could be gentle and firm at the same time.

The bidding opened at five thousand dollars and

quickly moved up until a woman started fanning herself with the program. The action startled the mare, who shied, then shook her head and pranced backward. The handler made the mistake of jerking impatiently on the reins.

At the rough treatment, the mare bared her teeth and nipped at the man. Dawn gasped as the handler struck the horse on her sensitive nose.

The owner, cursing both animal and handler, came into the arena, which further enraged the mare. She trumpeted and lashed out with her hooves at the two men who were menacing her while the crowd watched the drama.

Two mounted ring attendants had to come in and help the handler get the lunging mare under control. When order was restored, the bidding quit like a water tap suddenly turned off.

"Going once for ten thousand," the auctioneer finally said when it was clear no one would bid again.

"Going twice—"

He stopped and the crowd glanced around, wondering what was happening. "Ah, thank you, sir. I have ten thousand one hundred. Do I hear eleven?"

"He's pushing it," Hunter commented. "That horse is temperamental. It'll take an expert to handle her."

Dawn thought of Jackson. "She's smart. Perhaps if she were treated right, she'd be okay."

He looked doubtful.

No one wanted the animal. The man who'd bid ten thousand looked relieved when the mare sold for a hundred dollars over that. Dawn craned her neck but she couldn't spot the person who had bought the horse. She thought the new owner had gotten a bargain. Based on breeding lines alone, the mare was worth three or four times that.

After the auction, Dawn ambled outside with Hunter. The late-afternoon sun made her squint. "Let's go to the stables," she suggested on an impulse.

At the long row of stables, she paused at the mare's stall and glanced in. The animal was gone.

"I hope whoever got her knows how to handle animals," she said, unable to keep her disappointment hidden.

"You seem to know something about her."

"I saw her open the latch on the stall door." She laughed, remembering how smart the horse was. "She nearly got loose, but…a cowboy noticed and stopped her."

Hunter chuckled, too. "I'd hate to be the owner when he finds out she's capable of that. It's hard enough keeping stock where you want them without your horse opening gates behind your back."

Knowing how skilled Jackson was with animals, Dawn wondered if he could train the mare not to practice her trick unless instructed to do so. Perhaps he would have helped *her* train the mare. She wished now that she had bidden on the horse. She could have gotten a bank loan.…

She tried to shrug aside her regret. She hadn't the time to fool with a temperamental horse, or the money to buy a purebred Arabian. But the animal had been beautiful.

"It's time to get back to the hotel," Hunter remarked, glancing at his watch. "I have a dinner to attend. Sure you don't want to go and listen to a boring speech?"

She laughed at the disgruntled face he made. "Thanks, but I'll pass."

They returned to the hotel. The mothers were back from shopping and lunch with friends. The three women went to dinner together after Hunter left. Dawn searched the crowd but saw no sign of Jackson the entire evening. After a nightcap with Hunter when he returned, she retired to the room she shared with her mother.

In bed, she lay in the dark and explored the nagging disappointment she couldn't deny. She tried to talk sense to her heart, but it wasn't listening. There was only one voice it wanted to hear, and the voice of reason wasn't it.

Jackson heard the crunch of tires on gravel and knew Dawn had returned. He frowned, realizing he'd been listening all morning for the sound.

Down the road, he saw McLean remove luggage from the station wagon. Dawn and her mother went inside their home. McLean and his mother continued to the ranch house.

A whicker brought his attention to the horse in the paddock. The mare rose and pranced, pawing the air with her feet, her silver mane flashing in the noon sun. In the couple of days he'd worked with her, he'd already learned she was more show than bite.

"Good girl. Come here now. Come on, girl." He spoke in a low croon and held out a hand.

The mare crossed the temporary paddock he'd put up behind the cabin, her eyes bright with interest, but wary, as if suspecting a trick. He waited.

She inched closer, her neck stretched as far as she could get it, her nose quivering as she sniffed. He held his hand flat and steady, a sugar cube on his palm.

Finally, he felt the velvet-soft brush of her lips as she took the treat. She immediately backed away before pausing to crunch the sugar into powder in her strong teeth.

"Good girl," he praised her. "You're a fine girl, mighty fine." He finished hooking the wire of the temporary fence into place, then started another strand.

While he worked, he thought about Dawn. He wondered what she'd done in Reno for the past two nights, and if she and Hunter had danced. That thought made him angry, so he tried to avoid it and concentrate on work.

An hour later, he felt a touch on his shoulder. His gut tightened into a hard knot. He turned and stared into luminous golden brown eyes.

The mare snuffled at his hand, her pose wary, ready to bolt at the slightest hint of trouble.

Chuckling, he scratched the base of her forelock. "Liked that, did you?" He reached into his pocket and let her take another sugar cube. "Good girl," he praised her again. "You're going to be okay, you know that?"

He didn't believe in omens or anything except his own ability to take care of himself, but the fact that the mare had approached him without coaxing filled him with a keen sense of satisfaction and of good things to come.

Hearing a commotion near the creek, he studied the scene spread before him like a tapestry. McLean yelled orders to one of the cowboys who was working with the remuda, then jumped into a pickup. Dawn climbed into the passenger side. They tore out across the pasture after one of the hands hurriedly opened a gate to let them through.

Jackson went down to find out what was wrong.

"There's water flooding one of her fields," the cowboy explained. "The creek is running, but it ain't supposed to be, this time of year."

Jackson saw Russ come out of his house and head for a truck. He decided to join the party. He was inside the pickup by the time the foreman was cranked up and ready to go. Russ gave him a black look but didn't object to his tagging along.

They rode in silence to a reservoir that fed the stock tank in summer. While they did get occasional showers in the dry season, most of their water came from snow melt-off. The stored water became crucial during August and September to get them through the fall roundup.

Russ stopped beside McLean's truck. Jackson followed him to the spillway where Dawn watched McLean and Larry, the foreman's son, work at closing the sluice gate.

"There's a rock wedged in there," Russ reported.

Jackson saw the obstacle. "Steady me," he told McLean. Grabbing the gate handle, he held on while he stuck his foot over the edge of the concrete piling that supported the spillway and sluice. He felt a hand grab his belt and another his wrist. He kicked at the rock that held the gate. It moved a bit. He kicked it again.

"It's going. Try again," Russ encouraged from behind his right shoulder.

He gave it another kick, and the stone tumbled down the spillway along with the thousands of gallons of water they were losing. The two men pulled him back to safety.

McLean and Larry cranked the wheel. The gate slipped into place and the flow of water stopped.

"How the hell did that happen?" McLean turned a hard gaze on Larry.

The younger man shrugged defensively. "I don't know. I found it this way and tried to close it. I couldn't get it to budge. That's when I called Dad."

"Dawn found her fields flooded when she went out to check them and came to me," Hunter reported. His frown was ominous. "I want to know who did this. The gate didn't open itself."

Jackson felt what was coming in the silence that followed McLean's statement.

Larry nodded his head in Jackson's direction. "I saw him up here a couple of days ago."

Jackson tensed for battle. He was at a disadvantage here, three against one. And no one's word but his own.

"He wouldn't do something like this," Dawn spoke up. "This is his ranch, his water, his cattle. Why would he want to harm it?" She crossed her

arms over her chest and gave each of them, including
Hunter, a defiant glance.

He was hit with a powerful urge to make love to
her—right after he bawled her out for defending him
again.

"I can handle this," he told her. He looked the
three men over. "I was up here yesterday, taking the
starch out of a horse I'm working with. She needed
a good workout before she was ready to pay attention
to what I wanted her to know." He grinned, adrenaline pumping now, daring them to start something.

The foreman frowned when his son started to speak
again, then looked at McLean. The young man sub-
sided.

McLean studied the spillway and the sluice for a
long minute. "This has been open longer than a day.
I assume if you wanted to drain the reservoir, you'd
dynamite it and get the job done," he said in a sarcastic drawl. Giving a tight grin, he turned to the foreman. "I suspect some kids hiked through here and
wondered what would happen if they turned the
crank. Maybe we should keep it at the barn and bring
it up when we need to release some water. What do
you think?"

The foreman concurred and went to the truck to get
his toolbox and remove the wheel from the gate
mechanism.

Jackson watched the little drama play itself out. He
had a feeling he'd been set up, but there was nothing
he could do to prove it. He studied the men, managing
to ignore Dawn's smile and sympathy with an effort.

McLean and Russ were busy with the wheel crank.

The young cowboy wore a look of tight-lipped anger and wouldn't look his way. Yeah, he'd been set up.

"Looks as if you have things under control," he said. He glanced at Dawn. "Ready to go back?"

She hesitated for a second, then nodded. "Yes, I need to check the rest of the crops."

"Sorry about this," McLean said, pausing to cast them an appraising glance. "I'll see that the ranch makes good on any loss you have."

"That's okay." She started down the steep incline that formed one side of the reservoir.

Jackson fell into step beside her, ready to grab her if she slipped. They made it down without mishap. "Let's take the pickup." He pointed out the one he and Russ had used.

On the trip back to the main quarters, taken at a much slower pace than the one coming out, he tried to think what he wanted to say to her.

"I told you not to fight my battles," he said at last, not speaking until he'd parked the truck in its usual place next to the big barn.

"Speaking up for someone is not fighting their battles," she retorted, giving him an exasperated frown. "Besides, I agree with Hunter. You'd just blow the dam up if you decided to get rid of it."

He had to smile. "Is that what you think?"

"It's what I know. You're a full-speed-ahead-and-damn-the-torpedoes type. You were ready to fight all three of them up there." She made a tsking sound.

Her scent, spicy and sweet, filled the cab of the truck, reminding him of all the places he wanted to explore on her enticing body. Heat spread out in waves like radiation from a sun somewhere inside him. He inhaled deeply and tried to remind himself of all the reasons he should stay away from this woman.

She was a friend to his enemies. She had told him her love and loyalty lay with them. Rumor had it that she'd marry McLean. Hell, he'd seen her kiss the man. She'd gone to McLean before she'd come to him.

None of it mattered.

There was this moment and the heat and her spicy flavor and the fact that she had defended him. Twice.

He slid across the seat.

"Jackson?" Her voice was hardly audible over the rush of blood through his ears.

"Yes," he said, not caring what she was asking.

He was close now. She gazed at him, her eyes wide and wary, but unafraid. He caught a strand of her hair and wound it around his finger. Her breath fanned lightly over his neck, his chin and finally his mouth as she lifted her head.

Now.

He settled his lips over hers and felt the tremor pass from her to him and back again. For a moment he couldn't breathe, as if something heavy lodged in his chest.

After stroking her lips, he parted them with his tongue and tasted the sweetness inside. A fever took hold of him, burning him with needs he didn't want to admit.

She met his passion and gave it back, so rich and joyous in the giving that it unnerved him. No one had ever sent his mind into a whirl or stirred up emotions long since conquered and put away—until this woman. No one but his mother and grandfather had ever been there for him—until this woman. No one had ever taken his side without question—until this woman.

Then he could no longer marvel at the exchange of passion between him and her. There was only them and the fierce, hot desire burning brightly between them.

Their breathing grew labored. He pushed his hands under her shirt and found the smooth expanse of flesh. Even that wasn't enough. There were other places to explore, to touch, to merge into one sweet, throbbing flesh.

He ravished her neck. He caressed her breasts. "When it's like this, when there's only the two of us and you're sweet and smiling and ready for me, then life is good and I forget the rest—all the times it was hell."

In his voice he heard the ache and loneliness of times past when he'd felt betrayed by those he had loved and trusted. He took a breath and cursed silently until he had the feelings beat into submission. He tried to figure out how to take the words back, but nothing came to mind. He didn't want pity from her or anyone.

Dawn gazed at him with passion-dark eyes. Her pupils were so enlarged, her eyes looked like onyx outlined by pale blue rims. He forced his gaze from hers. She saw too much, this woman who watched and listened.

The noon sun glinted from every blade of grass so that the world seemed to glow when he looked around and tried to get his bearings. He had a sense he needed to get away, before... Before what?

Down on the road, he saw Margaret McLean out on one of her almost-daily inspections of the ranch. That sight was the dose of reality he needed.

"It's time to go," he said.

Dawn nodded, her eyes puzzled at the change. He clenched his jaw and helped her out of the truck. They walked without touching to where their paths branched, one way leading to his place, the other to her home.

A whinny greeted them, coming from behind the cabin.

Dawn gave him a questioning glance.

"Come on. I'll show you."

They went around the cabin and to the back. The silver mare whinnied again and shook her mane, then looked expectantly over the strands of barbed wire.

"The mare. You bought her? You were the one?"

He nodded. "She'll make a fine saddle horse for a lady. She's wary but she can be ridden."

He watched Dawn's eyes glow with pleasure. Her smile lit up the world. His heart clenched and unclenched, did rolls and flip-flops. He could feel himself grinning like an idiot, the world set right once more.

It was embarrassing for a grown man to be enthralled with a woman. This was sex—nothing more. He tried to scowl but couldn't.

"I'm so glad you bought her. You shouldn't have

done it, but I'm glad you did.'' As she murmured in a tone filled with wonder, she petted him, her hands running over his chest, his cheek, his shoulder, touching his hair.

He caught sight of Margaret on the ranch road, watching them with disapproval stamped all over her. He took Dawn's hand and set it away from him. "Watch it. We're being observed.''

"Observed? Oh.'' She caught sight of the older woman. A blush ran under her cool, pale skin.

Yeah, he'd read the situation right. Her response had been a passion of the moment. The same as his.

She said goodbye and raced down the slope, a sylph rushing to her destiny. He didn't think that destiny included him.

Chapter Eight

Dawn lifted her hand and knocked on the cabin door. The sound echoed inside, but didn't bring anyone to answer her summons. She tried again, then walked around back.

Jackson was there, mounted on the gray, putting her through her paces. Dawn stopped in the shadows and watched, admiration filling her for both horse and rider. Together they were a skilled team.

She waited until he'd finished before stepping up to the barbed-wire fence. "That was impressive."

He grunted an acknowledgment, swung a leg over the saddle horn and dropped to the ground. The mare nuzzled his shoulder. He patted her nose and gave her a sugar cube.

"You'll ruin her teeth," Dawn warned.

"And spoil her, too," he agreed. "You want to

take a ride and try her out?'' He pushed the mare aside when she nibbled on his ear.

Dawn grinned wryly. ''I don't know. She seems to be in love with you. She might resent another female.''

''You can handle her.''

''How do you know that?''

''You have the hands for it. Come on.''

She hesitated, then nodded.

He helped her mount, then walked beside the horse to the stables. When he had the stallion saddled, he led the way across the meadow toward the rolling hills that enclosed the north end of the valley.

Her heart beat in time with the thu-thump of the horse's hooves hitting the turf as he chose a path that took them high into the pine and redwood forest surrounding the ranch. The trail wound in and out of the trees, alongside the creek where she'd first seen Jackson.

''She rides like a dream,'' she called to him, pulling in close beside him. ''And handles like one, too.''

He gave her a very male, very satisfied smile.

They climbed higher, the path becoming steeper, until, forty minutes later, they came to a rocky outcropping that formed a bluff, a stubby ''finger'' that pointed directly into the valley. They stopped at the edge of the precipice.

Dawn drank in the beauty of the scene as if it were an elixir from the fountain of youth. The mountains rose around the ranch like a basket, holding the valley securely inside. A couple of jets had left contrails across the sky. The white plumes formed the handle of the basket, making the image complete.

She was aware of Jackson beside her and his steady gaze as he watched her take in the panorama.

"What were you doing at the cabin?" he asked when she finally looked his way.

"There's a barbecue at the lake this weekend. It's a fund-raiser for the school band to buy new instruments. I thought you might like to go."

"Why should I?" His scowl was not encouraging.

"To do a good deed for the community. To meet your neighbors." She paused. "To show you aren't afraid."

His eyes went as black as a storm cloud. "Afraid of what? A bunch of piddling ranchers and store clerks?"

The stallion stirred restlessly, catching his rider's tension. Jackson stroked the smooth neck.

"Afraid to be seen with me." She looked him in the eye, daring him to refute her words.

That puzzled him. "Why should I be afraid to be seen with you?"

She shrugged. "You implied I might find it difficult to be seen in public with you rather than Hunter. Since it doesn't bother me, I thought you might be the one who found it hard to face the stares of others." She gave him one of his hard-edged sardonic half smiles that dared him to accept her challenge.

"I stopped giving a damn about what people think a long time ago."

"Good. They start serving at six. I thought we

would leave around a quarter of. Do you want to pick me up, or shall I come by for you?''

He gave her a narrow-eyed study that should have shriveled her spine. She refused to back down.

"Look, angel face, I'm not your goodwill project for the year. You don't have to take me under your wing."

"I disagree."

He gave a huff of exasperation. "You'd drive a good man to violent acts."

"My mother often mentions something similar, only her reference is to saints and swearing."

"She has my sympathy."

"So will you be going with me?"

"Yeah. I'll try not to get in any fights."

"You'd better do more than try. I won't put up with any more brawls between you and Hunter."

"You'd better tell him that." He nodded down the trail. "Here comes Prince Charming."

Sure enough, Hunter was coming up the trail toward them at a rapid clip. He pulled up on the verge. "You been with that horse all afternoon?" he demanded, nodding toward the gray mare.

"Pretty much. What's the problem?" Jackson asked.

"Some of our young cows got in a field of locoweed. We'll probably lose a few and their calves. I'm trying to figure out how the gate was opened when nobody was supposed to be in that field until we got it sprayed out and sowed in pasture grass."

"It wasn't the mare. She's in a temporary fence behind my house until I figure out where to keep her.

She knows how to open the stable and paddock gates.''

Hunter cursed. "Actually, I was hoping it was her. Otherwise it has to be one of the hands who got careless.''

"Did someone suggest the mare did it?''

Dawn caught the edgy undertone in Jackson's question. His posture was deceptively relaxed as he leaned an arm on the saddle horn and watched Hunter with a lazy interest.

"Maybe," was all Hunter said.

"Then I suggest you check that person's whereabouts at the time of the mishap." There was no mistaking the cold contempt in his voice.

"I will." Hunter shifted his attention to Dawn. "Mom said she mentioned the fund-raising this weekend. You want to go?''

"Yes. I've already made arrangements.''

She glanced at Jackson, whose expression dared her to tell what those arrangements were.

"I've asked Jackson to accompany me so he can meet some of our neighbors," she continued.

Hunter's eyebrows jerked upward, then dipped down into a frown at this news. Jackson's did the same when he was unpleasantly surprised. So had their father's.

After boring a hole through Jackson and then her, in a piercing perusal, Hunter shrugged. "I hope you know what the hell you're doing.''

"I do.''

"If I find that mare opening gates, I'll shoot her,"

was his closing remark to Jackson. He nodded, wheeled the gelding and rode off down the trail.

"You'd better watch it," Jackson advised. "You lose his ma's approval, and you may lose him."

"Oh, shut up." She nudged the mare in the ribs and headed back down the trail.

"Just trying to be helpful." He was anything but.

"Innocence doesn't become you. You're trying to cause trouble. You *are* trouble," she amended. That brought a flash of white across his deeply tanned face. "Lord of darkness, indeed."

She urged the mare into a canter when they reached the meadow. Jackson caught up and rode beside her, the black horse and the gray matching perfectly, stride for stride.

A premonition crawled along her scalp. She envisioned the Four Horsemen of the Apocalypse, invisible but menacing, riding with them, hard on their heels as they raced for home. If she and Jackson were two and Hunter a third, then whom did the fourth rider follow? The one called Death?

The phone rang just as Dawn came out of her bedroom. Jackson was ten minutes late in picking her up, and she was wondering if she should check on him. Her mother answered in the kitchen. "It's for you."

The distinct note of disapproval told Dawn it was Jackson calling. The telephone company had been at his house earlier that week, so she assumed he was hooked up to one of the ranch lines.

"I'll pick you up in fifteen minutes," he said without a greeting after she answered.

"Fine. I'm ready."

"Good." He hung up.

She returned the receiver to the cradle, then checked her purse for tissues, money and lipstick. She collected a leather jacket from the hall closet. She'd need it later, when the sun went down.

"Are you going to the barbecue?" her mother asked.

"Yes."

"With Hunter?"

Dawn had known the moment was coming all week. "No. With Jackson. I thought it was time he met some of the locals and our neighbors."

Her mother assumed that tight-lipped look she got when Dawn wasn't behaving according to her standards. "You shouldn't encourage him."

Dawn assumed her innocent-as-a-spring-lamb expression. "Why not? It's a fund-raiser. His money is as good as anyone's, isn't it?"

"That isn't the point."

"The point being that he's the outsider, the bastard son who doesn't belong?"

"Don't get on your high horse with me. You and your father always took the part of the underdog, but did either of you ever think the underdog was there because that was where he belonged?"

Dawn considered. "You know, I never looked at it quite that way." She grinned.

After a bit, her mother returned it. "He might leave you with more than a few bugs in your hair," she said softly, giving Dawn a sober glance.

"He might break my heart," Dawn agreed. "It might be too late."

"Oh, honey."

Her mother looked so worried that Dawn was compelled to hug her and reassure her she'd be okay. A knock at the door sent a tingle up her spine and she hurried to open it.

Jackson stood on the porch, looking resplendent in boots, sharply creased jeans, a white shirt and a leather sports jacket. He held a gray Stetson in his hand. When he smiled, her heart fell right over backward.

"Good evening, Dawn, Mrs. Ericson," he greeted them when he stepped inside the door.

Dawn was proud of her mother. Whatever her personal feelings were, she had been raised to be gracious to a guest in her home. She spoke to Jackson and asked about his day.

He told an amusing tale about moving the mare to the stable where she immediately taught all the other horses to open the stall doors inside of half a day. He'd had to wire them closed for the time being.

Dawn and her mother laughed, then she picked up her jacket and indicated she was ready to leave. Her mom refrained from telling her to be in early and wished them a good time at the barbecue.

"You've grown," Jackson said, taking her arm when they went outside.

"Boots," she explained. She realized they were dressed almost identically in boots, jeans, shirts and jackets. Her shirt was blue, and she wasn't wearing a hat.

On the way to the lakefront community, she chatted about life on the ranch. She asked him about the cows that had gotten in the locoweed.

"I made them an emetic my grandfather showed me. It worked, and they seem fine."

"I'm glad." She settled deeper into the seat of the pickup and gazed at the sliver of moon showing in the sky.

"Don't go to sleep," he warned. "I might have to stop and see if I can kiss you awake."

"Then we would never get to the lake."

"Are you saying my kisses aren't powerful enough to wake up a Sleeping Beauty?"

She laughed, and it came out sultry, flirty... challenging. "Did I say that?" she asked innocently.

He didn't answer. They arrived at the lakeside community park without further discussion.

"What is he really like?" Jenny demanded, catching Dawn at the washroom after the meal.

She had invited Jenny and her date to join them at the picnic table while they ate. She'd introduced Jackson to the couple, reminding them that he was John McLean's son without putting an emphasis on it. Jackson hadn't objected, but she'd felt the tension in him at hearing his father's name.

"You planning on staying awhile at the ranch?" Steve had asked. He was a local banker's son, in the business with his father now that he was out of college.

"Yeah, I'm working with the horses," Jackson had

replied as if this was the only reason he had to be there.

Dawn told them about the mare. The discussion became general after that and covered the many topics of interest to ranchers and their bankers—weather, the price of beef and leather, government regulations. She felt the tension gradually leave Jackson.

Other couples and townsfolk had stopped by. She'd introduced all of them to Jackson.

"He's wary," she answered Jenny's nosy questions as she washed her hands and reapplied her lipstick. "He was hurt when he learned his father had another family, just as Hunter was when he learned of a half brother."

"Is he Indian?"

"Half, I think. His grandfather was on one of the reservations over in Nevada."

"He looks so deliciously dangerous. Collette is going to be mad as a cat in a burlap bag when she finds out he was here and she missed him. She decided not to attend the picnic. 'Too provincial' was her term." Jenny laughed, delighted at having one up on their friend.

Dawn wasn't sure she'd have liked Collette on hand, making eyes and flirting outrageously with Jackson the way she did with all newcomers to her orbit. On the way back to the table, she worried about the state of her heart.

While she trusted Jackson completely to take care of her, she didn't think he'd be as gentle with her heart as he was with her person. He'd made it clear he didn't want entanglements of a permanent nature.

Forcing herself to be bluntly honest, she admitted he might want her mostly because he thought Hunter did.

The thought had lingered in her mind for days. It bothered her now even as she returned to the table, and they laughed and talked with others for another hour. The stars were out when they said good-night and climbed into the pickup.

"That wasn't too bad, was it?" she asked.

"It was okay."

"*I* had fun," she persisted.

"It was okay."

"Didn't you have fun?"

"It was—"

"Okay," she finished, then sighed.

"I had fun," he finally admitted. "Where was Mc-Lean? I figured he'd be around."

"I don't know. He usually comes."

"With you?"

"Lately, yes. When he and April dated, my mother would make them take me. I was the kid who tagged along." She laughed, remembering how it had annoyed her older sister, but Hunter had always been kind. He'd adored April.

"So why did you make me come tonight?"

"Make you? Ha."

"All right, why'd you ask me?"

"If you're going to make a place for yourself here, you should know the people. We all help one another when things get tough. Everyone has rough patches to get through."

He drove in silence for a ways, but she noticed the

hard set of his features. Apparently he didn't like the implication that he might be the one needing help someday.

"When I want friends, I'll choose them," he said in an icy tone.

She sighed. "I know. You don't need anyone. Right now. But someday you might."

He snorted.

The moon, still a sliver in the night sky, hung low over the horizon like a silver promise. She snuggled down in the seat, her knees propped on the dash, while dreamy visions took hold of her mind.

"Did I pass your test?" she asked.

"What test?"

"The one you give to everyone you meet. You're always testing people, daring them to knock the chip off your shoulder, pushing them to see how far they'll go, then standing back and watching their reactions. You did that to me in Reno. Did I pass?"

Jackson recalled her kiss when they'd stepped off the elevator. She'd surprised him and sent him into a spin that still had him dizzy. She'd asked him if he was ashamed of being with her. Damn fool question to ask a man, if anybody wanted his opinion.

"Yeah, with flying colors," he said, maintaining a sardonic edge with an effort.

With her nearly lying down in the seat, he wanted nothing so much as to pull off into a secluded spot and make out like a couple of schoolkids. More than make out. He wanted to go all the way, to find the hot core of her that lived demurely beneath that cool Nordic exterior.

"Good." Her tone was brisk, as if they were discussing the national debt or something equally interesting. She yawned, then chuckled. "It remains to be seen if you'll pass mine."

Now what was she talking about?

"Women," he muttered. "No wonder no one has ever figured you out. You talk in riddles."

"Then riddle me this—what walks on four legs, is the most boneheaded critter on earth and isn't worth the time it takes to train 'em to civilized ways?"

He turned onto the ranch road, but didn't stop until he reached his cabin. He parked in the shadows beside the lean-to and turned to her, resting his left arm on the steering wheel, his right along the seat so he could touch her hair.

"Okay, I'll bite. What?"

"The McLean brothers. One's as hardheaded as the other."

The blood rushed to his head so fast he saw red. He clasped her shoulders and brought her upright, his nose no more than three inches from hers. She returned his gaze without a qualm.

"Don't link me with him. We share nothing more than the haphazard sowing of a few wild oats—"

"Half the same gene pool," she corrected. "That's something else you're going to have to do—forgive your father for his mistakes. He paid a price, too."

"His wife paid the highest price of all," he snarled as she hit sore spots he thought had healed years ago.

She stroked his jaw, then cupped it and ran her thumb over his cheek. "So you do feel compassion for people. You keep your feelings so hidden, it's sometimes hard to tell.'' Then she smiled as if he'd done something she was proud of.

"Hell,'' he said, unable to take any more. He kissed her.

To his surprise, she didn't hold back but wrapped her arms around him and held him with a fierceness that stunned and excited him. The passion flamed high and sudden and nearly out of control.

"We'd better slow down,'' he said at one point.

Her hands were under his shirt, moving all over him. He wanted her to touch him everywhere.

She leaned her head against his chest. "I don't want 'slow.' I want *now*. I can't believe I said that.'' Her laugh was shaky.

He was trembling, too. Passion had never been like this. He reached inside and found the anger he'd lived with for years and yanked it between them as a barrier. He set her away from him and scooted back to his side of the truck.

She watched him for a long minute, neither of them speaking, then said, "Someday you're going to have to confront your feelings and figure out what they are.''

"Such as?''

"Are you going to live with hate and distrust all your life, or are you going to let the past go and find a future?'' Her voice was as soft as moonglow.

"You tell me.''

She toyed with the fringe on the front of her jacket. Finally she shook her head. "You have to find the truth in your own heart. My truths might not apply to you.''

"Your truths? Are yours different from mine?"

"I don't know." She opened the door and slipped out.

"Get in. I'll take you home." No woman had ever walked home on him.

"I'll walk." She moved off into the dark.

Dammit, she'd done it again—made him feel guilty for something he didn't even know he'd done. He slammed out of the truck and started after her.

A voice spoke out of the dark beside the stables. "You okay?"

"Yes," she replied.

He saw McLean fall into step beside her.

"What are you doing out?" she asked him.

"Tending a sick cow."

He heard her ask about the animal. They continued talking as they walked down the road. Two old friends, easy with each other. He was sure they'd never been lovers.

Hot flames licked through him at the thought. Truths? He'd tell her one. He was going to be her next lover. And that was a fact.

He walked into the empty house and heard the echo of his steps reverberate through the darkness. He steeled himself against the onslaught of loneliness he often felt at odd moments. He had the feeling it had been a mistake to come here to the McLean ranch. And that it was too late. He just didn't know for what.

Chapter Nine

"Be careful," Dawn said, knowing it was unnecessary, but unable to keep from voicing her worry.

"I will," Hunter assured her. He snapped the rifle closed and shoved it into the holster attached to the saddle before taking J.J. from her.

Dawn watched as Hunter tickled his son on the belly, then nuzzled the soft skin on the boy's neck. J.J. squirmed away from the caress.

"We'll be back in a day or two," Hunter said, giving the child back into her keeping. He hesitated, then leaned over and kissed her on the mouth.

She felt the question behind the kiss—a question she couldn't answer. She gazed worriedly into his eyes when he lifted his head. J.J. patted her cheek. "Say bye-bye to Daddy," she coaxed. "Can you say bye-bye?"

J.J. gave her a solemn stare.

"Okay, let's wave." She stepped back and lifted her hand when Hunter mounted the big gelding. He and Larry were going to try and find the cougar that had moved in. One of the area rangers would join them. With a tranquilizer dart, they should be able to subdue and transport the big cat to a remote area of Yosemite.

She and J.J. waved vigorously until the two men rode past the stables, then she returned to the house. Margaret and her mother were inside, chatting over coffee and rolls.

"Mmm, those smell good. I thought I detected homemade cinnamon buns baking this morning. Anna must have gotten up before dawn."

The housekeeper came into the room with fresh coffee. "Actually, I put them on right after breakfast. That's why Hunter and Larry were late getting started. They had to have a few to sustain them on the trail."

The women laughed at her droll smile.

"I hope they get back today," Margaret said, concern replacing her laughter. "I always worry when the men have to stay out overnight."

"They'll be okay. They can sleep in the snow hut if they have to spend the night," Dawn reminded her. She broke off a piece of roll and gave it to J.J. before taking a bite. After they'd shared the treat, he wanted down.

She set him on his feet. He immediately went for the whole plate, both hands reaching for the goodies.

Dawn laughed and caught him up into her arms

again. "I think this young man and I will go for a walk. Maybe I can tire him out for his morning nap."

The three older women thought that was a good idea. They resumed their gabfest when she left.

After changing J.J.'s clothing, Dawn headed outside with him. Going through the kitchen, she noticed the pan of rolls cooling on the counter. A thought came to her.

"Hold on, buddy," she advised. She scooped up four rolls, secured them in a plastic bag, then held out her hand. "I've got the loot. Let's get out of here."

Holding hands, she and J.J. walked onto the patio, then across the lawn. At the stables, she guided them around the paddocks, then up the incline to Jackson's home.

"Hello," she called at the door.

The solid oak door was open. A storm door had been installed. She peered into the dim interior of the kitchen. No one was at home. She thought she'd seen Jackson go inside when she'd been saying a farewell to Hunter.

"Looks like no one is here." She couldn't hide her disappointment from herself. Her days were too entirely caught up with thoughts of this elusive male.

"Don't give up so fast," a laconic voice replied.

Jackson came to the door. He was barefoot and wore jeans, but nothing else. She knew because the jeans weren't snapped or zipped. An enticing vee of male flesh drew her eyes down to the opening.

"You're staring," he advised as he opened the storm door. A half smile kicked up the corners of his mouth.

"I don't get to see many naked men this early in the morning," she instantly retorted.

J.J. pulled at her hand.

"This handsome fellow is J.J.," she introduced them. "J.J., this is your uncle. Can you say hi to Uncle Jackson?"

J.J. looked Jackson over in his usual solemn way and didn't utter a sound. Jackson gave her a quizzical glance.

"He's the silent type," she explained.

"Yeah, I heard." Jackson dropped down to his haunches. "We need to get down to basics." He thumped himself on the chest. "Me Jackson, you J.J." He thumped J.J. on the chest with one finger.

His mocking half smile bloomed into a real one, lighting up his bronze face the way the sun lit up the mountains each morning.

Dawn ignored the hitch in her breathing and watched the two males who studied each other as if waiting for the other to draw first. It was a standoff.

Then J.J. reached for the package of rolls. Dawn let the child take them. He handed them over to Jackson.

"He's decided you're all right," she informed Jackson. "How about a glass of milk to go with them? Shall we eat here on the porch?"

"Sure. Make yourself at home," he invited.

Within two minutes, he brought out a cup of milk and two mugs of coffee. He'd put on a shirt and socks and zipped his jeans. They sat on the porch, J.J. between them while they ate, and observed the cows and horses in the pastures. The mare was in with the black.

"Are you breeding her?" Dawn asked, surprised.

"Yes. Any reason why I shouldn't?"

She shook her head. "I assumed you'd work with her more before you decided to keep her. You are going to keep her, aren't you?"

"Yes. I want to see what we get from her and the black. With their coloring and conformation, the off-spring should be striking."

His eyes delved into hers. She thought of children, his and hers. Her nephew gave an impatient tug on her shirt and made a throaty sound. She tore another piece of roll off hers and handed it over. She was dismayed to see that her hands trembled slightly.

"What are you thinking that has you in a twitter?" Jackson demanded, reading her much too easily.

She pushed straying locks of hair behind her ears and smoothed them into place. "Of children," she confessed. "Ours. And what they would look like."

His expression hardened into stone. He swallowed but said nothing, just stared into the distance as if this moment didn't exist.

"Would they look like J.J. who has my family's blue eyes and your family's dark hair? Or would they have the McLean eyes with blond hair? Either would be a striking combination. Of course, green eyes with black hair is very attractive, too."

"I suppose you'll find out when you and McLean marry."

She breathed deeply as anger stirred. "Hunter and I aren't going to marry."

"That goodbye scene down at the stable looked pretty convincing to me."

Dawn shrugged, refusing to dignify that remark with an answer. She stopped J.J. when he reached for another roll.

Jackson realized she wasn't going to deny the homey scene he'd witnessed earlier. Shrugging, he handed over the last bite of his roll to the kid.

J.J. flashed him a solemn grin, grabbed the treat and stuffed it into his mouth all at once.

Dawn let her nephew climb down the steps and explore the yard. He gathered pinecones into a pile. When the stack was tall enough, he kicked it until all the pinecones were scattered, then started over.

"Life should be so simple," Jackson muttered, aware of the woman beside him with every cell in his body. She was dressed in shorts and a T-shirt. Her feet were in sandals. Her fine blond hair was pulled back into a ponytail with a red rubber band. She wore no makeup.

He was also aware of the kiss McLean had given her before he left that morning. It had looked very cozy—her holding the child, the man kissing both of them before leaving. Very definitely a family affair.

Something about the scene had jarred him. If he hadn't arrived at the ranch almost two months ago, she would probably have agreed to marry McLean by now. She and McLean might have already tied the knot—

"What's gotten you into a rage?" she asked, breaking into the dark thought.

"You," he said bluntly, causing her to blink those

incredible eyes and look troubled. "You love McLean and his kid. Why won't you marry him?"

"I'm not *in love* with him."

The quietly spoken statement dropped into his gut with the explosive power of a grenade. "How do you know?"

She turned from watching the kid. Her eyes met his and held his stare without blinking. He looked away.

"I think we have to find out what's between us first, don't you?"

He grabbed a handful of hair and watched it cascade over his fist as he released it. "Sex. I think that about sums it up. To you, I'm someone different."

"And what am I to you?"

More than I ever dreamed of. He crushed the ridiculous thought. "Mostly trouble," he said.

Her peal of laughter caught him off guard. He frowned, but it didn't bother her at all. He noticed her lips were enchanting when she laughed. They curved and lifted, outlining her mouth and the honeyed heat he knew he would find inside.

He joined in, but his chuckle didn't come off as cynical as he wanted. In fact, it sounded downright despairing—the way he felt sometimes when he thought of her in association with any other man.

She leaned close, her shoulder brushing his, searing him with the white heat of longing that turned his dreams into fiery storms of lust and need. When the kid looked at them, she clapped her hands.

"Good, J.J., very good. Can you find Aunt Dawn

a flower? I love yellow flowers.'' She pointed out some wild mustard growing at the edge of the yard.

The boy ran across the clearing and tugged off a bloom. He rushed to bring it to her.

''Oh, that is so pretty. Thank you.''

J.J. dashed off to pluck more blossoms.

''Why doesn't he talk?'' Jackson asked.

''We don't know. He scores in the normal range on all his skills except verbal. He can understand and follow directions, but he won't speak. Hunter has taken him to the university for testing. He's healthy and bright. He can make sounds. The doctor advised giving him time.''

''Maybe he needs a dog.''

Her eyes gleamed like moonstones. ''That may be the very thing. Is his uncle Jackson thinking of getting him one?''

He gave her a narrow-eyed scrutiny. ''I think I'm being roped in on that one by an expert.''

She beamed at him. ''I'm going on a trail ride tomorrow. Would you like to go?''

''Are you asking me for a date?''

''Mmm, yeah.''

''Okay. You want the mare?''

She shook her head. ''I need to take one of the cow ponies I'm training. She has a few rough edges.''

He gazed at her slender figure. ''Right. I'll be at the stables in the morning when you're ready.''

She called to J.J. and, hand in hand, they wandered down the road, pausing often to look at butterflies or flowers or a shiny rock. The woman and child reminded him of life and all the good things it used to hold....

"You're moody," Dawn remarked as she and Jackson crested the ridge that overlooked the valley. From here, she could see Highway 395 winding like a silver ribbon through the desert country east of the valley.

"I'm thinking," he said, correcting her.

"Men always say that. You deny having any emotions. I say you're introspective, maybe sad. So what gives?"

"Women are nosy, always prying into a man's thoughts. What happened to privacy?"

She laughed, delighted to have gotten a rise out of him. He'd been as silent as a rock on the ride. "Look at the sun glinting off Honey Lake. It looks like diamonds in the choppy spots but like pools of silver where the water surface is smooth."

"Yeah, silver," he repeated.

But when she looked at him, he was watching her. A pleased blush warmed her face. She gave him an oblique glance, then studied the lake again. It came to her that she was flirting with him. When she looked again, he was still watching her with that intriguing moodiness in his eyes.

An electric buzz sped along her nerves. She felt wary and nervous and excited, all at the same time. An aura of tension radiated between them, each feeding the other, until she was as tightly strung as piano wire. She drew several deep breaths, but it did no good. The sensation remained.

She watched the sway of his body in the saddle as he took the lead over the rock-strewn crest. His mount was a mare from the ranch remuda while she rode the cow pony she was training. Both animals had good instincts.

"Next week, I'll start teaching this one to go home if something happens to her rider. Do you want to work together on any of the ranch horses?" she asked.

Jackson twisted around in the saddle. His eyes seemed shockingly green in the dim light under the canopy of pine trees. He seemed to consider everything she said as if looking for a hidden agenda. His caution made her question herself constantly.

"That might be a good idea," was all he said.

Her grimace was directed at the back of his head.

"You might freeze like that." He chuckled while she snapped her mouth closed.

She grinned and relaxed, glad she'd suggested the outing even if she did wonder about her own motives. She stayed alert while her mount picked its way over the rock field.

From there, the trail wound west among the trees again. They followed one of the numerous creeks that existed only if there was enough snowpack to keep them running. This one was only a sliver of water compared to three months ago when she'd ridden this loop.

Jackson pulled up in a shady spot that enticed them to stop and rest before heading back. She hobbled her horse while Jackson dropped the reins of his in a ground hitch. The ranch mare would stay close unless spooked—then she would head for the stables where she knew food and safety awaited.

"It's fun having someone to ride with," she told him. "I've always ridden alone up here."

"Why didn't McLean come with you?"

"I never thought to invite him. He's been so busy since his father died. Before that, I didn't think of it." She wished she hadn't mentioned the father, but the words spilled out before she thought.

Jackson didn't acknowledge her slip. He nodded, then settled on the grass with his back to a fallen pine. The horses drank from the creek, then started munching on the long blades of summer grass.

"Deer sign," Dawn said, pointing to the droppings at the edge of the glen. She sat on a huge boulder and wrapped her arms around her knees. The silence sank into her.

"There was bear sign all along the trail. Wild game is increasing throughout the mountains."

"Yes. I wonder if the forestry department will bring the wolf back the way they've done in Yellowstone to help control the deer population."

She considered the consequences of having "live-in" wolves, so to speak, then studied Jackson, who appeared to be napping although she couldn't tell for sure. His hat was pulled down over his forehead so she couldn't see his eyes.

In spite of nature documentaries, people seemed to think of the wolf as a loner, an animal who prowled silently through the world. She knew that wasn't true. The wolf was a pack animal, very sociable and very vocal. And very caring of its young, even offspring not its own.

She'd seen those traits in Jackson when he'd shared his roll with J.J., then asked about the child.

Or was she reading in traits she wanted him to have?

He pushed his hat off his forehead and gazed into her eyes. She realized he'd been aware of her scrutiny.

"I need a drink. How about you?" he asked. At her nod, he rose and retrieved a water bottle from his saddlebag. He left his hat hanging from the saddle horn before bringing two apples over and offering one to her.

He sat on the rock beside her. They shared from the bottle of water, then ate the apples. He tossed the cores to the two horses who pounced on them as if they were manna falling from heaven. She laughed as the animals eagerly searched the grass for more.

Jackson reached over and traced one finger along the line of her throat. Her laughter dried up. She jerked around to stare at him, her eyes widening as she looked into his.

"I told myself all the reasons I shouldn't do this over and over on the ride up here," he murmured. His gaze paused at the vee of her shirt.

"What are they?" Her heart pounded so hard she thought it would seriously bruise itself against her ribs.

His laughter was brief and not amused. "You belong here. You have family and friends. I'm the outsider."

"You think of us as enemies." She heard the sorrow in her voice and felt it echo deep inside.

"You're likely to be the death of me," he conceded, "especially if McLean finds us. Or maybe your mother would shoot me if she knew what I dream every night."

"I dream, too," she admitted in a low voice.

"Are yours about us, just you and me, alone in a shaded glen like this one and the world far away?"

She recalled all the erotic visions that chased through her head whether it was night or day. "Sometimes."

He drew a deep breath, held it, then let it go. "Then let's find out if dreams do come true."

His touch was neither gentle nor tentative. He took her mouth as if he knew the moment wasn't going to last and they had to take all they could while they could. The kiss was urgent but not frantic. Never that.

He was as skillful as a lover as he was at handling the ranch horses or the stallion and silver mare. His tongue glided smoothly into her mouth, coaxing a response she was all too ready to give. One hand slid behind her. The other stroked up and down her arm.

A moan clawed its way from her throat, giving voice to needs she'd tried to ignore for days and weeks.

He pulled her against him. She came willingly, her hands thrusting into his thick hair. He pushed her hat off and pulled the band from her hair, causing it to tumble over her shoulders. Restless, he ran his hands into the strands and let them slide through his fingers.

It was an act more erotic than any she'd experienced in her lifetime.

"God, I love your hair," he whispered as he dropped a thousand kisses along her temple and ear. He took her earlobe between his teeth and caressed it with his tongue.

She sighed, her breath catching in her throat as if it were a sob rather than a sound of ecstasy. She held his face captive between her hands and sought his mouth. He didn't withhold himself from her, but gave her back kiss for hungry kiss until they were breathless.

When she could bear it no longer, she unfastened his shirt and tugged it from his jeans.

The longing increased. "I need you," she told him and trailed frantic kisses all over his chest, then pressed her face against his warm, solid flesh.

She raised her head and gazed at his lean, muscular torso. He had very little body hair—only a sprinkling in the middle of the chest and surrounding the tiny nipples tanned to dark brown by his days in the sun.

He lifted her and stepped from the rock to the ground. Gazing past her adoring eyes, he walked to his horse. "The blanket," he murmured.

She freed it from the saddle. He returned to the rock and set her down on it. He spread the blanket on the ground and held out a hand to her. She met his sultry gaze without a quiver. She knew—they both knew—what would happen if she accepted his silent invitation. She stepped forward.

"I have protection," he said in a tone so low she could barely hear him.

She nodded, then sat down abruptly, her legs refusing to hold her any longer.

He lowered himself beside her, then gently pushed her onto her back. His chest half covered her when he bent to kiss her again. His hand glided between them, and she felt his fingers on the buttons of her shirt. Then it fell open.

"Let's get this off. I want to see you." He made short work of her bra, removing it and her shirt before covering her with his own body again.

She slipped her arms around him and caressed his back, loving the feel of him, so smooth and strong, the muscles rippling under his skin as he shifted over her again. All doubts dropped away. This was right and good.

His leg slipped over hers. She caught it between her thighs, holding him tight.

"Oh," she said as he began caressing her with his entire body, pressing and withdrawing, moving slightly from side to side until her blood sang in her veins and a wildness invaded her.

"I've wanted you like this since that first day in the woods. You came to me. We shared food. You belonged to me from that moment. I knew it...."

She moved her head restlessly, not in denial—she was beyond something so simple as denial—but with need as her hunger grew. When he moved slightly, she followed, her body surging under his like a storm-driven sea.

"I'm not leaving," he assured her. "I couldn't."

His hand went to the snap at her waist. A second later, her jeans were open. His hand was deep bronze against the pale skin of her abdomen. She could only stare as he eased it inside her clothing. She wanted him to move faster.

He splayed his fingers, kneading her flesh the way she'd seen him soothe a horse or rub out a sore spot. She arched her neck and bit at him—soft love bites that encouraged him to do more.

"I'm trembling," he said huskily. "I'm trembling because this might not last, and I think I'll die if I don't have you this one time, and yet I'm almost afraid to touch you. You're forbidden—"

"No, not to you…or only if you choose it."

She pulled his mouth to hers and kissed him as ardently as she could. She felt him sigh, then he explored farther until he found the hot, welcoming center of her. She moved to the stroking of his sweet invasion and loved the feel of his arousal against her thigh.

"Please," she murmured, over and over. "Please, yes. Now, yes. Please, Jackson. Yes."

"Let me see you. I have to see you."

He sat up and, in an easy movement, stripped her shoes and jeans, then the rest of her garments from her. She helped him do the same, their hands meeting, blocking, interfering, but finally it was done.

She feasted her eyes upon him while he did the same to her. It was wonderful and delicious.…

"And frightening." She gave voice to the thought.

"I would never hurt you," he vowed, lifting his head when he would have kissed her.

"Not you. Me," she said. "Us. The way I feel. It's so strong and urgent and tense so that I think I might scream if you don't...if you don't...kiss me right now."

This time when he guided her to a reclining position, he followed and covered her completely, his body snug against hers everywhere, his legs meshed with hers so that she felt his arousal against her abdomen, felt its throb and the pulsing demand to be inside. She moved one leg, and he did the same, slipping both his between hers.

He positioned himself for entry, but didn't proceed. "Wait." He found his wallet and prepared himself.

She watched as he held himself up on his arms so that they touched only at the apex of their legs.

"That's incredibly intimate," she whispered. She was startled to hear how shaken she sounded.

"Don't be afraid. I... We can stop at any time. All you have to do is say the word."

Her trust in him, which had been complete, grew apace with her love. "I feel as if I'm blooming inside, as if all of springtime were inside me."

"It is." His voice was guttural, sexy.

"Come to me."

He took a breath. She knew he was reaching for control. So was she. He moved slowly into her. She held her breath and realized that he was, too.

When the joining was complete, they both sighed as if some great feat had been accomplished.

He sank onto her, holding his weight carefully on his arms. His lips touched her cheek, her hair. "Beautiful," he said in that same throaty tone. "Beautiful and warm, heaven and hell and everything in between."

She heard the wonder and the agony, but she didn't have time to think about it. There was only them and the moment. She wept a little. "No one has ever spoken like that to me," she explained when he paused to study her.

"I could tell you other things, but it would only make it harder when I leave."

She scarcely heard the warning. "Now, my love. Now, please."

He gave her everything she had ever dreamed of.

Chapter Ten

Dawn roused from her dreamy state when Jackson stirred beside her. She lay snug against his body, his arm over her middle, one leg over hers.

"That was lovely," she murmured, happy and surfeited by their lovemaking. He'd come to her twice during their lazy sojourn there in the glen.

He lifted himself on an elbow and studied her face. "You're in the afterglow," he commented. "Don't go thinking it was more than what happened."

She laughed. "I am in the afterglow. I'm thinking I'm in love with you. I've thought so for weeks."

"Sexual satisfaction can be pretty mind-bending," he told her bluntly. "I wanted you. You wanted me. That's as complicated as it needs to get."

"You wish." She sat up and stretched, aware of his eyes on her breasts as she lifted her arms over her head. Her nipples tingled as she remembered his kisses that had rained all over her.

"I'm different from the local boys you've known all your life. That's all. A year from now, you'll be married to Hunter or someone just like him."

"Or maybe I'll be married to you." She lifted one eyebrow and dared him to contradict her. "My mother and all my friends have warned me away from you."

"They're right."

"No, they're not." She gathered her clothing and leisurely dressed. She yawned. "Are you going to invite me to spend the night?"

"No." He pulled on his clothes at a much faster pace than she did. He folded and rolled the blanket when she stepped aside and tied it behind his saddle.

"Stubborn," she muttered, but without heat. She was still floating in the magical world they'd created. She basked in the knowledge that they would come together again no matter how much he fought it.

She checked the girth on her saddle before swinging up. He mounted, his expression closed. His gaze flicked to her.

"Are you all right?" he asked, his voice lowering, lingering in the cadences of the passion they had shared. Whether he wanted to admit it or not, he was a man who cared deeply for the others in his life.

Her heart skipped around inside her at his concern. "Yes, wonderful."

He gave her a repressive frown, but nothing could bring her down from her cloud. It was late afternoon before they arrived at the ranch. She stopped by the

McLean paddock and leaned toward him. He hesitated for only a fraction of a second before catching her behind the neck and giving her the kiss she had silently asked for.

"See you," she told him and prodded the mare into a trot. She had chores to do.

To her surprise, he came with her. He fed and watered her boarders while she cleaned her mount's hooves, then brushed the chestnut's hide until it gleamed. She moved their small herd of beeves from one field to another.

When all the tasks were finished, Jackson stopped beside her. His gaze was introspective and troubled.

"You're still glowing," he murmured, lifting her chin with a crooked finger and peering into her eyes.

"I can't help it. This afternoon was wonderful—"

"It was sex."

She touched his face, loving him so much she wanted to do something wild and fierce. "Don't be sorry," she said softly. "Don't make me sorry."

She smoothed the troubled lines from his forehead. His chest moved in a deep sigh as if he didn't know where to go from here. He shook his head and swung into the saddle, heading back to the McLean ranch to do the chores there.

Dawn watched him until he disappeared into the stables, then she walked toward the lighted windows of her home. Her mother was on the phone when she went inside.

"Was that Hunter with you?" she asked.

"No. What's wrong?"

"Hunter's horse returned to the ranch a couple of

hours ago. Margaret just found out Larry went with the ranger while Hunter followed some tracks on far ranges of the ranch. He thought there were some poachers after deer. I heard two voices when you came home. I'd hoped you'd found him.''

Alarm swept through Dawn. ''No. That was Jackson. He helped me with the chores.''

Her mother's frown stopped a further confession that they'd been together most of the day.

''There was blood on Hunter's saddle, according to Russ,'' her mother continued. ''Margaret thinks Hunter was hurt. Maybe someone tried to kill him.''

Dawn felt the suspicion behind the words. ''Not Jackson. He wouldn't hurt anyone.'' She headed for the door. Grabbing her jacket on the way out, she called back, ''Tell Margaret I'll get Jackson. I know the area where Hunter was supposed to be. We'll find him.''

She checked the sun's position. There was plenty of light. It wouldn't be dark until after nine.

''Jackson?'' she yelled, bounding up on his porch. The light was on in the kitchen. She went inside. She heard the shower and followed the sound.

The addition to the cabin appeared to be finished, she noted as she walked down the hall. Golden oak trim formed a lovely contrast to off-white walls. Deep green carpeting reminded her of a mossy path through the woods.

The water switched off.

''Jackson,'' she called again.

The door at the end of the hall opened. He stood there, water beading on his shoulders, a towel wrapped around his waist. "What are you doing here?" He didn't sound very welcoming.

"It's Hunter. His horse returned without him. There was blood on the saddle. We have about three hours of light left. Do you think you could track him?"

"Sure. Indians are born knowing how to track."

"The way women are born knowing how to type," she retorted. "I haven't time for a fight. Are you coming with me or not?"

A moment passed. "Let me get dressed," he said and disappeared, closing the door behind him.

She returned to the kitchen. An insulated bottle sat on the counter. She prepared hot soup from a can and poured it into the thermos. If Hunter had been out all night, he'd need warmth, inside and out. She went to search for a blanket.

"We'll take my truck," Jackson said, encountering her in the hallway. "I have a blanket and first-aid kit in it."

She nodded. "I'll call Margaret and see what's been done. Russ might be going out." She dialed the number.

"No," Margaret reported. "We haven't decided on anything. I talked to the sheriff. He says by the time they got the dogs over here, it would be dark and they would have to wait for morning. Search and Rescue will go out at first light if we haven't heard anything by then."

"Jackson and I are going out now. I know the area. We might find him before nightfall. I have the cell phone. Call if you hear anything."

Jackson picked up his jacket and rifle. He loaded a box of shells into his pocket. Shortly after that, they headed for the hills again, this time on an old logging road once used by the forestry department to reach a fire lookout.

"He'll be okay. He's resourceful," she said at one point during the silent drive.

Jackson flicked her a glance, but didn't say anything. She fell silent. When they reached the lookout, she told him to stop. "This is where the ranger was supposed to meet them. The road hasn't been kept up beyond here. The cat was in this area, so they probably didn't have to go far."

"Cover your ears," Jackson advised. He removed his rifle from the carrier and stepped away from the truck. He fired three times into the air. They waited five minutes, but no call or shot answered them.

"They went this way," she said, pointing to fresh hoofprints in the dusty road.

Jackson studied the ground. To the side of the road he found the big paw prints of the cougar. The men had followed on horseback. Three horses had headed out. Only two sets of prints returned. He got the first-aid kit, then he and Dawn trailed after them.

"Here's where they caught the cat." Jackson pointed to the boot prints surrounding the place where the cougar had dropped after being tranquilized. He figured they had loaded the creature onto a horse to take it back to the ranger's truck at the lookout.

Another set of hoofprints led off through the chaparral. He followed them. Dawn stayed close behind.

"The light's gone gray," he said. It was almost

impossible to follow the horse's imprint in the hard grit along the old mountain trail. Only the entrenched ruts kept them on track. They came across horse scat a little later that was no more than a day old.

"That had to be Hunter's mount."

"Or the poacher's," Jackson said.

"He's okay," Dawn said, determination in her voice that it would be so.

Jackson fired into the air again. The three shots echoed between the mountain peaks. When they died away, he heard a faint but distinct shout.

"This way," Dawn urged, running down the road. "Coo-ee!" she called.

The call came back to them, but in a masculine voice. They followed the sound until they found Hunter resting against a tree. His bandanna was tied in a tourniquet around his thigh. He smiled when they came up. "About damned time."

Jackson stayed back, his eyes alert to any movement in the woods around them. Dawn knelt beside McLean and put a hand to his forehead. "What happened?" she asked, her manner dripping concern and sympathy.

"I believe I caught a poacher. He didn't stay around long enough to ask, though. He must have thought I was a deer. The shot came out of the blue. The horse bolted and I fell off like some kind of greenhorn." He shook his head in disgust. "I tried to walk out this morning, but the bleeding got too bad. I figured someone would be along soon if I stayed on the road."

Dawn inspected the wound. "The bullet must be inside. There's no exit hole."

"Yeah," McLean agreed with a grimace as she probed the area. He sucked in a harsh breath when Jackson knelt beside him and tucked a pressure bandage under the bandanna.

"Let's get him to the truck," he said to Dawn. Hell, he would be willing to take a potshot, too, for a little of that loving attention from her. Squelching that thought, he checked the bandanna and saw the bleeding had stopped.

Together Dawn and Jackson got Hunter to his feet and supported most of his weight until they reached the truck. They put him in front between them and started the trip back to the ranch. Dawn fed him the hot soup.

"God, that's the best thing I ever tasted," McLean murmured. He laid his head against the back of the seat.

Jackson remembered her preparing soup for him when he was injured from the fight.

"Poor darling," she crooned, again feeling his head. "He doesn't seem to have a fever," she said to Jackson as if he'd asked for a report on the man's condition. "When did you get shot?" she asked McLean.

"An hour after first light this morning. Yesterday, I found a trail and followed it until it was too dark to see, then bedded down for the night. I heard a shot this morning and rode this way."

"Oh, Hunter, you could have been killed."

"Naw, I'm too mean for killing, sweet pea."

Jackson watched a smile bloom on her lips. A surge of hunger darted through him as he recalled kissing those lips until he was sated, then coming back for more. He found himself annoyed by her concerned attention to McLean.

"Are you cold?" she asked solicitously.

"Yes."

Jackson could feel the tremors in the other man and experienced a jolt of guilt over the jealousy he couldn't deny. McLean had probably been in a state of semishock for hours. "There's a blanket behind the seat."

She pulled it out and tucked it around McLean, making worried sounds like a mother hen...or like someone who cared deeply for another.

"Take him straight to the hospital in Reno," Margaret ordered after checking Hunter's condition. "I'll alert the surgeon you're on your way."

"Don't need a surgeon. The doc at the clinic can take the bullet out," Hunter insisted.

"I think you should go to the hospital," his mother said.

Dawn almost smiled as they argued. Taking care of hardheaded ranchers was no easy job. They all seemed to have their own ideas.

"Why don't we let the local sawbones see him?" Jackson suggested. "He can tell us if we need to go to Reno."

"Good idea." Dawn was sitting beside McLean who was now laid out in the back of the ranch wagon, his injured leg surrounded by an ice pack. It had started bleeding again with the removal of the tourniquet. "Anna, call Dr. Wilson and tell him we're on our way."

"You should come with us," Jackson said to Margaret. With that piece of advice, he lifted her from the wheelchair and placed her in the front seat. He folded the chair and stuck it in the back. "Ready?" he asked.

"Yes," Dawn said, more worried than she let on.

Hunter was pale, his pulse thready and his breathing shallow. Only pure cussedness had kept him alert thus far, she was willing to bet. She had no idea how much blood he'd lost. Infection might be a problem, too.

The four of them arrived at the clinic just as the doctor drove up. A light was on inside. Dawn could see the nurse at the window. The woman had the door open by the time they brought Hunter inside. He'd refused the gurney and was walking with minimal support.

But not without pain, she noted. The sweat was beaded on his forehead by the time they reached the examination table. The doctor washed up and donned a jacket and rubber gloves before checking the wound.

"Yep, it's in there," he said cheerfully. "Let's get the leg X-rayed before we start digging."

By the time that was done, Hunter was looking decidedly on the ragged edge. An IV dripped into his arm. The doctor stuck the X ray on a light screen on the wall and checked the angle of entry. He gave

Hunter a couple of shots, then began the probe with some long-handled tweezers.

Hunter gave a grunt of pain.

"We've got it," Dr. Wilson proclaimed jovially. He was a man who loved his work. He gave a yank and the bullet slid out of the engorged flesh with a fresh spurt of blood. "Let's mop it out and get it closed," he told the nurse.

She handed him a gauze pad, then brought a tray of suture needles for the doctor's selection.

Hunter turned an interesting shade of green, gave a groan and passed out.

"Good," the doc said, smiling. "This next part will be easier if he's asleep." He finished up with several neat stitches in the torn leg, checked the IV solution, explained about the antibiotics going in with the glucose, and assured Margaret that all was as good as it could be.

"I'll keep him here tonight. That leg is going to be sore as hell tomorrow, but you can tend him at home as well as we can here. You can pick him up around noon."

"I'll stay here tonight," Margaret decided. "In case Hunter needs something."

The doctor pointed out that the nurse lived next door and had a listening device from the patient's room to hers. "Besides, he's going to sleep all night after what he's been through. And probably most of tomorrow, too."

"I'll stay," Margaret said firmly.

"Let me," Dawn volunteered, sensing a storm

brewing. "I can sleep right here in the room. Just in case," she added at the doctor's frown.

"Good, that's settled, then," Margaret said so fast, Dawn realized this was what the woman had wanted all along.

She glanced at Jackson, but he watched the scene with that impassive expression he often wore when around the McLean family. He was clearly the outsider.

The doctor shrugged, then wrote instructions on Hunter's chart. He and the nurse moved the rancher to a hospital bed in a room down the hall from the examining room. A monitor was hooked up so that his vital signs would be displayed at the nurse's home. An alarm would go off if Hunter took a turn for the worse.

Dawn sat on a small sofa in the patient's room. The nurse gave her a blanket and a pillow.

Satisfied that her son would be seen to, Margaret wheeled toward the door. "We can go now," she said imperiously.

Dawn touched Jackson's arm. "Thank you for helping me find Hunter."

"Nada," he said, shrugging off her gratitude.

"I thought it was something," she contradicted. Leaning into him, she kissed him on the mouth, then shooed him out the door. "See you tomorrow."

She was aware of Margaret's disapproval as Jackson wheeled the woman to the station wagon and helped her inside. His eyes met hers briefly before he drove away. The closed expression left her puzzled.

Too tired to figure it out, she made sure Hunter

was covered, then settled herself for the night on the sofa. She didn't awaken until six when the nurse came in with coffee, fruit and muffins.

"I thought you might be hungry by now. I know you get up early on the ranch."

"Yes, thanks. I didn't get any supper last night. We forgot about it in the excitement of finding Hunter."

"He's still sleeping like a baby. I'll start him on another IV. When he's had that, he should be able to go home. He was lucky you found him when you did. A night of being out in the cold in his condition and his chances wouldn't be so good."

"I was worried about that while we were looking," Dawn admitted. She stood by the bed while she finished eating, tenderness in her heart for this man she'd known and loved all her life.

Margaret called at eight to check on her son. The report was good. Hunter was sore, but he had no fever. He could go home. Jackson arrived at eleven to pick them up.

Hunter grumbled about having to use a wheelchair, but Dawn thought he was secretly glad. He grimaced each time he had to move his leg. They put him in the back seat so he could sit with his leg straight.

The doctor provided a pair of crutches. Jackson stuck them in the rear, then climbed into the driver's seat. Dawn sat in front, too, but partially turned so she could keep an eye on Hunter.

The trip to the ranch was accomplished in silence. At the house, Hunter insisted on using the crutches to hobble across the patio deck and into the house. She and Jackson helped him up the stairs.

"Thanks for your help yesterday," he muttered, his gaze resting on Jackson with a troubled expression.

Jackson nodded and left while Dawn settled the patient in bed and gave him a pain pill. She tiptoed out.

Downstairs, she encountered a crowded tableau on the patio. Jackson and Russ were there. So was Russ's son, Larry. Her mom had come up and stood close to Margaret and Anna. The sheriff and a deputy were seated at the table.

"How is he?" Margaret demanded when she stepped out.

Dawn glanced around the patio. Vines grew over the trellis that shaded part of the patio from the August sun. The dappled light shifted in lazy patterns when the leaves shimmered restlessly in the breeze. The peaceful scene was at odds with the tension she sensed.

"Asleep. The doctor said he would probably sleep most of today. He gave me some pills for tonight. I left them on the kitchen counter," she said, glancing at Anna. "We're to continue the antibiotics until they run out to make sure there's no infection. He had cloth and debris in the wound for several hours."

No one commented on her rather lengthy explanation.

"What's going on?" she asked.

"Larry has some information on who shot him," Margaret said in a hard tone. "The sheriff came out

when I called. I wanted all of you to hear this. Larry,''
she said, indicating the ranch hand should speak.

"Well, I, uh, saw someone. Maybe. It was kinda
dark there in the woods.''

"What did you see, son?'' Russ prompted.

"A man with dark hair. Riding a dark horse.'' He
looked directly at Jackson.

She saw Jackson's stance shift as if he readied himself for battle. Anger speared right through Dawn. "If
you're implying it was Jackson who shot Hunter, it
wasn't.''

"Can you account for yourself yesterday morning
early?'' the sheriff asked Jackson.

Dawn waited. He said nothing. Then he shook his
head. She cast him an impatient frown. Why didn't
he tell them he'd been with her?

"I can account for him,'' she announced.

She defied any of them to say different as she
glanced from face to face, noting her mother's shock
while the others looked disapproving or carefully ex-
pressionless. Jackson's muscles pressed against the
skin of his jaw as he set his chin in anger. With her,
she saw.

"We went for a ride. He left the stallion here and
rode one of the ranch mares. I rode one of my boarders. Night before last, his pickup never left the ranch.
It was in its usual place yesterday morning when I
got up.''

"He could have gone by horseback—''

"At night? Through the mountains?'' She gave a
huff of disgust at Margaret's suggestion. "Hunter was
shot at dawn. Jackson were here at the ranch.''

"Dawn," her mother began, worry in her eyes.

"He was with me most of yesterday," Dawn continued. "He didn't look or act like a man who'd been riding the hills all night." She gave Margaret a stern look. "We all want to find out who did this to Hunter—we came close to losing him—but blaming innocent people won't solve anything." She glared at Larry.

"I saw what I saw," he stated belligerently.

"What you thought you saw or wanted to see."

Jackson stepped in front of her. His glare was as fierce as the noon sun. "Forget it," he said. "They've made up their minds." He stepped off the decking. "I'll be at my place if you want me," he said to the sheriff.

The lawman nodded and let him go.

"You arrest him and you'll have me to deal with," Dawn said. "He was with me yesterday. He helped me find Hunter."

"How'd he know where to go to look for him?" Larry demanded, looking triumphant.

Dawn realized the younger man resented Jackson. It was Jackson who had discovered the ranch stud was injured and taken over the care of the remuda. It was Jackson who'd known what to do for the cows who had gotten in the locoweed. But it was always Larry who claimed to have seen Jackson in the area when anything went wrong.

"Any poachers would have come up the old logging road from the other side of the mountain as far as they could," she added. "They would stay close to their truck if they were planning on carrying out meat. That's why Hunter went that way. That's why *I* searched in that direction.''

She stared the young cowhand straight in the eye. He shuffled uneasily and looked away.

"Dawn.''

She looked at the sheriff.

"You willing to swear Jackson McLean was with you?''

She nodded. ''He was at the stables when I went out to take care of our stock. We finished the chores and left around ten. I'm training a cow pony to trail-work.''

The sheriff nodded.

"Hunter thinks one of the poachers thought he was a deer and shot before getting a good look at him. He says it was an accident.''

"That would be my guess,'' the sheriff agreed. "Well, we'll move along now. Tell Hunter to call and give a statement tomorrow or when he feels up to it.''

He and the deputy left. Russ motioned to his son. "You'd best be getting back to work.''

Larry turned red under his dad's scrutiny and hurried out of sight. He cast Dawn a glance that sent a shiver down her spine. He was furious with her.

"I have work to do, too.'' She left the house and headed for her place before she said things she would regret. Margaret had wanted Jackson to be guilty. She probably thought she could get rid of him that way.

Jackson caught up with her near one of the greenhouses. The three hands were out in the field. He pulled her inside and gripped her shoulders, giving her a little shake.

"Dammit, I've told you not to do that," he said in a low growl. "You didn't need to give me an alibi."

"I told the truth. What did you think I would do? Let them arrest you?"

He let her go and impatiently raked a hand through his hair. "They couldn't have arrested me. They had nothing to go on, not even circumstantial evidence. You didn't have to involve yourself."

"I *am* involved. In case you've forgotten, we were together up there on that mountain most of the day."

"Yeah, a thing you would be better off to forget. You shocked the moms with your announcement. Keep that up and you'll lose McLean."

She was shocked that he could think of her with another man after their day together.

"There's no future for us," he said harshly, reading her mind. "You belong here. I don't."

"You could," she said stubbornly.

"Not in this lifetime. Right now you're wrapped up in romantic ideals, but when the shine wears off, what would be left? You'd be separated from the home and family you've known all your life. Then the hatred would grow and fester."

He walked off and left her standing there, her love for him a lonely ache in her breast.

Chapter Eleven

"September the fifth," Dawn said to Hunter. "The year is two-thirds over and I barely remember it starting."

"Watch it. That's a sign of old age, I've heard. Of course, I wouldn't know personally."

She wadded her napkin and threw it at him. He tossed it back. He stretched his injured leg and flexed it carefully. This was his first day without the crutches. He was looking fit and hale. She recognized signs of impatience. A man used to hard work and action, he didn't like the enforced rest.

Shouts from the pasture stopped the conversation. The men were moving the first load of calves, which were prime beef yearlings on special contract, onto trucks. Jackson was in the forefront, directing the work.

He had taken over the operation of the ranch while Hunter recovered. It had happened so casually, Dawn didn't think the men realized how much and how often they turned to Jackson for orders.

"Looks at home in that saddle, doesn't he?" Hunter remarked, his eyes narrowed as he watched.

Dawn nodded. "Like you, he's a natural leader." She considered whether she should say more, decided against it, then did it anyway. "Russ is almost sixty. I've noticed it's getting harder for him to climb on a horse." She paused.

"You think he wants to retire?" Hunter asked.

Obviously the idea hadn't occurred to him. Russ had come to the ranch when Hunter had been a toddler. Anna had already been employed here to help Margaret with the active child and the ranch work the previous year. The two had married and become a part of the place.

"I don't know. I do know it isn't going to work out with Larry and Jackson both here. If Jackson decides to stay, Larry will have to go. He resents Jackson."

For the past ten days, Jackson had been working on the ranch from dawn until dark. He hadn't stopped even to say hello to her once during that time. She knew from Anna that he'd gone to Reno to deliver some designs to a small local company that owned a silver mine and specialized in Native American jewelry. But he hadn't bothered to tell her.

She was curious about that side of him—the artist as opposed to the warrior or tough rancher—but he showed it to no one. He was skillful with his hands, whether using them at his craft, on the horses...or on her.

Heat surged into her face. She tried not to remember their day on the mountain, just the two of them, and the magic between them.

"Are you in love with him, sweet pea?"

She turned an anguished gaze on Hunter. "Yes. More than I ever dreamed possible." She begged his forgiveness with an imploring look.

"I recognized the signs." He sat lost in thought for several minutes. "It's the way I felt about April. As if the sun didn't come up until I saw her each day. It was funny how it happened. One day I looked up and there she was, riding one of the meanest horses in three counties and laughing while your mother fretted and your father cheered. She nearly ran me over. After I got done wanting to shake her teeth out, I wanted to kiss her senseless. You know?"

"Yes, I can identify with that." Dawn laughed ruefully. She had wanted to take a rock to Jackson's hard head more than once. She wasn't sure why he was avoiding her, but she thought it had something to do with Hunter being injured.

Men had an odd sense of honor at times. She knew Jackson wouldn't take advantage while his enemy was down and out. Therefore, he had to wait until Hunter was on his feet before he could come to her again.

Maybe that was why she'd invited Hunter out on the patio to watch the cattle loading—so Jackson could see his half brother was walking on his own.

She sighed.

"I think we could have a good marriage, but I won't lie to you," Hunter continued after an introspective moment. "I'll never love anyone the way I did April. Part of me died when she did."

She squeezed his arm. Everyone had adored April with her quick laughter and delight in life. "I know. I loved her, too. She was a wonderful sister. She mended my clothes so Mom wouldn't know I'd torn them climbing trees or riding a horse I wasn't supposed to."

"Maybe it's just as well you and I didn't marry. You would have been cheated of the wild excitement of sexual awakening. Don't blush. I've seen that, too. It was the same between me and April as it is between you and Jackson. And maybe between my father and his mother."

Dawn blinked as tears filled her eyes. "You've finally forgiven your father."

Hunter heaved a heavy sigh. "Yeah. Love isn't something that can be easily ordered into place. I hate it that he hurt my mother, but I understand it."

"You seem to have accepted Jackson," she ventured, marveling at Hunter's mellowed tone.

"It's hard to hate a man who saved your life. As hard as it is to admit, I think he has a right to be here. He's making a place for himself." He pushed himself upright. "Come on, walk the old man down to the action. I can't sit here while there's work to be done."

She strolled across the lawn with him. He took it slow and walked with a limp, but he didn't need support. Jackson glanced their way when they arrived at the fence where the loading chutes were. His gaze was impassive and opaque.

"If he's what you want, demand marriage," Hunter said with a wicked gleam in his eye. "That's what April did."

"Really? Didn't you want to marry her?"

"Sure, but I was still walking around in a daze that she'd been under my nose all those years and I hadn't realized it. You women have to clue us fellows in."

Dawn laughed at his droll humor, her eyes on Jackson.

Hunter chuckled. "Go get him, gal."

"I think I'll have to." She made up her mind to have a showdown with him that night.

Bathed, dressed in blue slacks and a white shirt, she meandered along the trail to Jackson's place. The sunset shot fingers of magenta and gold through the pink-tinted clouds nestled on the horizon.

The breeze played hide-and-seek through the trees, now in front of her, now behind her, catching at her hair and tossing it over her face, then sweeping around and blowing it straight back.

She tugged her jacket closer around her. The air had a nip of fall in it, growing rapidly cooler as the light faded into deep twilight. She was pleasantly tired but peaceful.

The harvest was in, for both the herb business and the ranches. Rolls of hay were stacked along fences. Bales of alfalfa were stored in barns. The long hiatus of winter would soon blow in on the northwest wind.

She wanted things resolved between her and Jackson before the first snow.

So she had decided to take the bull by the horns. Bullheaded men were in that class, she had decided. She smiled and walked faster, eager to see him up close and, if she had her way, very personal.

The first thing she heard when she stepped up on the porch was a flurry of yelps from inside. Jackson had gotten a dog? A young one, judging by the sounds of the barking.

The door opened before she could knock.

"Oh, how darling!" she crooned.

The pup, a black Lab, stuck his nose against the storm door and wagged his tail so hard, his entire body swayed. He gave a couple of welcoming yelps.

Jackson scooped one hand under the rounded belly and held the pup so its paws cleared the floor while he opened the storm door and let her in. The pup paddled furiously but to no avail.

When Jackson had the door securely closed, he released the puppy who barked and dashed madly around her in circles, dropping wet licks on her ankles as he did. She tried to pet him, then waited until the burst of energy was over before lifting the little demon into her arms and scratching his ears. Then she noticed a cat—a fully grown yellow tabby—sitting by the table, licking her paw.

"You've started a menagerie," Dawn said.

He cocked one dark eyebrow as if questioning her common sense. "The pup isn't for me."

"Then who— Oh! For J.J.?"

He nodded. "All kids need a dog."

"And the cat?"

He shook his head in disgust. "She's a barn cat who decided she preferred being a house cat. She followed me home the other day and refuses to leave."

"Hmm, a tactic that may be worth evaluating," she murmured wickedly.

Jackson saw she wasn't going to be put off by his ill humor. The truth was, his heart was going like a downhill freight train. She'd only have to touch him to know his indifference was a lie.

"It was kind of you to think of J.J. I think a dog will be the very thing for him."

He shrugged to indicate the subject was of little importance to him and tried not to notice the way Dawn's eyes gleamed at him as she petted the pup. He walked over to the counter, picked up a brandy snifter and took a sip. He needed to keep his distance and a cool head around this woman. She was the one person who could make him forget all about survival and live for the moment.

"Is this a social call?" he asked cynically.

"No." She stood, her eyes never leaving his. "I'm sorry that Margaret tried to get you blamed for shooting Hunter. She encouraged Larry to say it was you."

"Her feelings toward me aren't any secret. At any rate, it doesn't matter. McLean cleared me."

The next thing he knew Dawn had her arms around him and was kissing him as if there was no tomorrow. He couldn't move, couldn't breathe for a few seconds; then his thinking processes shut down entirely as sensations and emotions he'd tried to forget burst through him.

There was only the feel of her, of her slender body pushing against his, searing him at a thousand points of contact—breasts, belly, hips, thighs. She melted into him, a warm, flowing material, shaping itself to every angle and plane of his body, touching him in places he hadn't known existed before she came into his life.

He uttered a groan of need, the ache of hunger so great it racked his body with a kind of pain that no instrument of torture could match, and he knew he wasn't going to be able to turn her aside. It was too late. He'd already clasped his arms around her, holding her so tight he trembled with the effort at control.

"Kiss me," she murmured, her lips skimming his eyes, his cheek, his mouth.

Inhaling deeply, he drew the scent of her into his lungs. Her spicy sweetness made him dizzy.

He caught her head between his hands and held her still while he took her mouth in an endless kiss that burned right down to the center of him. He fought himself, her, the brevity of time, the sense of life slipping beyond his grasp if he didn't take her right this minute....

"Dawn, no," he said, pushing the word out on a ragged growl. But he couldn't push her away. To set her aside was beyond his strength.

"Yes," she said, her voice so husky with desire it sent a new rush of blood through him. "You're wonderful and I love you." She leaned her head back. Her straight blond hair fell like a cascade over her shoulders.

Her breasts burned against him. He could feel the

beaded tips, could almost taste the honeyed smoothness of her body on his tongue.

"I love you," she repeated, looking at him as if he were the most wonderful thing she'd ever seen.

He closed his eyes, but she refused to be shut out. She moved against him. His body, ever eager for her, surged with painful urgency, demanding relief in her hot depths.

"I can't... I have to... I want to see you," he said, giving up the struggle, knowing he couldn't win against her allure. "Once more," he whispered, burying his face in her hair. "Just once, if that's all I can have."

"Forever," she vowed. "We can have forever."

Her tongue invaded his mouth with sweet purpose. She stroked his body with hers, his tongue with hers. The kiss became a contest and a confrontation as well as love play between them. He knew he wasn't going to stop—not now, maybe never....

"Love me," she crooned. "Jackson, please, love me."

"I do," he said, his voice so hoarse with need for her he hardly recognized it. "I will."

Driven by sheer desperation, he lifted her and carried her into the bedroom he'd prepared. For her, he now admitted. The house had always been for her.

For this woman he couldn't have.

The knowledge tore at his insides until his heart felt raw and bloody from battles long fought and long lost.

The pup followed them into the room. Jackson

scooted him outside with his foot and closed the door. This night was theirs. He wanted no interruptions.

"Once more then," he said, laying her on the bed.

Never taking his eyes off her, he threw his clothing aside. She watched him, her eyes large and dark, luminous in the moonlight that flooded the room.

He placed one knee on the bed and, leaning over, unfastened her blouse, then the pale blue slacks. He slipped her sandals off, then the pants. She raised her hips, helping him when he indicated she should, watching, her eyes bright with anticipation, dark with passion.

By the time she was naked, he was shaking, near the end of his control. She surged upward, melding flesh to flesh, driving him closer to oblivion. He sucked in a calming breath and reached for the pull on the bedside drawer. "Wait."

She saw what he was doing and took the packet from him. She tore it open. Her fingers trembled with the intensity of her love as she covered him.

"When you touch me like that, you drive me right to the edge," he warned. "It's never been this way with a woman."

"How?" She reached between them and cupped him in an intimate grip that had him gritting his teeth and hanging on to his sanity by a thread.

"Hot. Urgent. Worse than a schoolboy. I have no control where you're concerned."

"You don't have to have control. I want you. I want you now. In me. I want to feel you...."

He couldn't hold out any longer. He came into her with one quick thrust and felt the sweet welcome of her body, hot and wet and ready for him. He found her mouth and thrust with his tongue. She answered with undulating rolls of her hips against his, moving with him in the ancient rhythms as endless as time itself.

She said his name over and over and clung to him, wild in his arms. Driving him closer and closer to ecstasy with her response.

He stroked her breasts, then down her body to the golden curls at the apex of her legs. She twisted slightly and he found the passionate center of her. He stroked until she moved like a storm-tossed sea beneath him. When she went still, not even breathing, he let himself ride the tide of release with her.

When she pressed her head against his shoulder and sobbed quietly, he went over the edge, thrusting fiercely until every drop of passion was wrung from him. His energy spent, he collapsed and felt her make slight adjustments under him to take his weight. He shifted to the side.

"Don't go," she murmured, turning with him so they stayed together. She sighed.

"I couldn't."

If someone had knocked down the door, he couldn't have stopped them at that moment. But that was something he wasn't going to confess. He'd already proved what a weak bastard he was where she was concerned. He hadn't meant to make love to her again. Not ever.

"We shouldn't have done that," he said after a while, when he could speak again.

She kissed across his chest and teased one nipple

with little licks of her tongue. "Why not? Didn't you like it?"

He heard the lilt in her voice and knew she was in the afterglow again. He didn't look into her eyes.

"Yes." He could admit that much. "It only makes it harder when it's time to leave."

She stiffened. "Are you going to leave?"

"I've been here all summer. McLean is on his feet. He can take over. The remuda is in good order. The hands will have the strays rounded up and down from the hills in another week or two."

"What about your house?"

He shrugged. "It'll be here when I come back. Maybe I'll spend the summers up here. It's cooler than in Reno."

"Is that where you live?"

"I have an apartment there. I spend time in the desert or the mountains when I've had enough of the city."

"Do you visit the reservation?"

"Not since my grandfather died."

"Then why do you have to go?"

He was aware of the movements of her breathing and the warm pressure of her thigh across his. "Because."

His body stirred with renewed vigor and hunger. He tried to ignore it. Where she was concerned, it was a losing battle. When she tightened the internal muscles, his body sprang to full life again, eager to play this game of passion with her.

"You're asking for trouble." He frowned when she smiled and thrust delicately against him.

"Why didn't you come to me?" she asked.

"I've been busy."

"Not that busy. I live a quarter mile down the road—the same one you use to go to town or the mailbox." She nipped him on the neck, then blew on the spot, punishing and teasing him at the same time for his neglect.

He thought of the restless nights of thinking about her. When he slept, his dreams were of them and the day they'd spent on the mountain. He resorted to anger.

"What's the problem? Isn't McLean's company enough? Do you have to have all the men within sight at your feet?"

She huffed indignantly. "What men? I only see one stubborn male in the vicinity." She stroked down his side with her fingernails, then across his belly.

He clenched his teeth while hunger roared through him as if he'd not sated himself with her only minutes ago.

After a bit, she sighed, then tilted her head back so she could study him. "I told Hunter I was in love with you."

"Hell," he said.

"He said he'd seen how it was between us and that I should go for you if that's what I wanted."

"He's as crazy as you are." He rolled over her, giving in to the urge to satisfy the hunger once more, before—

"I want you to stay," she said.

The simple statement almost made him forget the truth he'd known for weeks and had admitted when they found McLean on the trail. He decided to tell her.

"Look, what you feel—what we share—is passion. It's mind-blowing, but it isn't...what you think. If I hadn't come along, you'd have married Hunter by now. You two have everything going for you—the kid you both love, the ranches that fit together, the lives and memories you've shared. When I'm gone, you'll forget—"

"Damn you." She struggled beneath him.

Her thrashing about only incited him more. He pinned her arms above her head, then stared into her eyes until she stopped glaring. He knew she didn't understand that their passion was a thing of the moment. What she'd shared with Hunter formed the basis for a lifetime. He'd faced that truth when Hunter had been injured.

His mother had maneuvered Dawn into spending the night at the clinic. On the ride back to the ranch, she'd pointed out all the reasons Dawn and her son belonged...and he didn't.

But he hadn't needed the sermon. He'd seen for himself. Dawn had been all loving concern, her touch so tender it hurt while she cared for the other man. He'd seen the trust and love between them over and over that summer. He'd been insane to think...to dream of them...

But he was over it now.

Except he was going to take this one night. It would be his forever, to lock in the corner of his heart, to cherish on cold nights when the wind howled and loneliness ate at him until he wanted to howl, too.

Still looking into her eyes, he began to move. She pressed her lips together, then bit on the bottom one as passion grew and bloomed between them again. When she moaned and moved to his rhythm, he felt no sense of triumph.

He kissed her gently yet fiercely, feeding the hunger even as he satisfied it, knowing he wouldn't find the depths of passion ever again with any woman but this one.

Dawn woke alone in the king-size bed. Her slacks and blouse were neatly laid over the back of a chair covered in buttery-soft buff leather. Here, as in the rest of the house, oak trim added warmth to the white walls. Huge beams crossed the vaulted ceiling and a fan circled lazily overhead. The sun shone through pleated shades.

She rose, showered, and dressed in her slacks and shirt. Jackson was in the kitchen, sitting at the table with a mug of coffee before him on the table.

"Good morning," she said, her throat tightening so the words came out very sultry. The puppy leaped around her feet, causing her to trip.

Jackson caught her before she hit the floor. "Damn menace," he muttered.

"Me or the pup?" She grinned at him, so deliriously happy and lighthearted she was in danger of floating right up to the sky if she went outside.

He made sure she was steady on her feet, then set her aside. "You want eggs and bacon for breakfast?"

"Yes. Whatever you're having."

He cast her a glance that had her insides curling at

the edges. "You should leave. McLean won't like it if he sees you up here."

"You called him Hunter last night and once before." She sipped his coffee and patted the puppy on the head.

He scowled and slapped slices of bacon into a skillet.

"You've mellowed since you've been here," she continued, taking his seat at the table. "You came here for revenge, to show Hunter and Margaret you couldn't be run off a second time. Now you know them as people. It makes a difference, doesn't it?"

His snort didn't dismay her.

"That's one of the reasons I love you." She scratched the cat's ears. "One of many reasons."

The tension sizzled louder than the frying bacon. He turned to her, his expression harsh. "Last night was passion, nothing else. You belong here—with McLean."

"I prefer to make my own choice. Hunter isn't it. He knows that." She studied his closed face. "You are. And there's nothing you can do to change it."

"I can leave. You'll forget—"

"Don't make me face that."

The muscles worked in his jaw. He flipped the bacon pieces over and got three eggs out of the refrigerator. He put four slices of bread into the new toaster on the counter and set them to browning.

They didn't speak while he finished preparing the meal. He brought the plates to the table and put them down none too gently. She saw they were still the same old ones the cowboys had used when the cabin had been a line shack—the same ones she'd played house with as a girl.

"We'll need new dishes," she said, voicing the inane thought that came to mind.

"You and McLean?" He plunked a mug on the table, refilled it with coffee, pushed it at her, retrieved his own, filled it and returned to the counter. On his next trip, he brought the napkins and silverware.

Those, she saw, were new.

"Firebird, McLean—whatever name you want to use." She gave him glare for glare, then spoiled it by smiling.

They ate in silence. He finished first and watched while she spread jelly on her last section of toast.

"Does your mother know where you are?" he demanded.

"I'm sure she does. I told her I might be out late when I left last night. She knew I was coming to you."

"You've probably blown your chances with McLean," he informed her coolly.

She finished, patted her mouth on the napkin, then rose. "I've got work to do." She considered her words carefully. "If you really think last night was a mistake, I'll go and not bother you again. I do love you, but I'm not good at living with uncertainty."

"It was a mistake." He seemed suddenly tougher and harder than she'd ever seen him.

She breathed slowly, deeply, knowing how close she was to shattering. "Well, I asked," she said.

She pushed the puppy aside so she could get to the door. The pup danced around her feet and latched on to her sandal strap. She had to get him to let go before she could leave.

Jackson made an impatient sound and scooped the pup up in one hand and held it against his chest. She slipped through the door and walked across the clearing into the woods. This time, she didn't look back.

Chapter Twelve

"What do you think?" McLean asked.

Jackson looked at him blankly.

"I said, do you think we should put up a stock shelter?" He pointed to one in a catalog.

Jackson shook his head. "You've made it okay without one so far."

He glanced down the road. Dawn was in the training ring, working with a young girl and her horse on barrel racing. He was acutely aware of her presence. For the last hour, he'd been listening to her voice giving out orders and encouragement to the teenager. Now her laughter rang out, drawing his eyes that way.

McLean slapped the catalog closed. "Why don't you go down there and say hello or kiss her or something before you get a crick in your neck from looking that way?"

Heat rushed into Jackson's face. "Why don't you mind your own damn business?" He saw Mrs. McLean out on the patio. Anna and J.J. were with her. This was the chance he'd been waiting for. "I've got something for the kid."

He dashed up to his house and grabbed the pup from the pen he'd made to keep it from chewing up what little furniture he did have.

The cat followed them out. When he strode across the yard, she stayed with him. He stopped the pup from chewing on his shirt collar.

McLean had joined the women on the patio. "There's coffee and rolls," he said, giving Jackson a somber look.

Jackson saw the old lady stiffen, but she said nothing. There was no use borrowing trouble. "No, thanks."

He knelt on the decking in front of J.J. and set the pup on its feet. It checked out J.J.'s sneakers.

The kid looked amazed and turned big blue eyes to him. The pup sniffed J.J.'s coveralls, then got a whiff of cinnamon and sugar from the roll the boy was holding.

Before Jackson could stop him, the pup had snatched the roll from the kid and gulped it down. He then proceeded to prop his paws on the boy's chest and lick his face.

J.J. hugged the pup.

Jackson looked questioningly at McLean. The other man made no protest.

"Well, that's the easiest washing I've ever seen

him take,'' Anna commented as the pup finished cleaning the sugar from J.J.'s face.

Jackson relaxed. He rose and pulled a booklet of instructions from his pocket and dropped it on the table in front of McLean. ''This tells you how to handle the pup.''

''Thanks.''

The cat jumped into Margaret's lap. The woman's hands flew up in surprise. The cat circled, then lay down. A loud purr filled the air when Margaret stroked its fur.

Jackson figured the cat had found a new home. Smart animal. It knew which side its bread was buttered on, and living with a half-breed bastard wasn't it. Crossing the lawn, he glanced down the road toward Dawn's place. His heart leaped into his throat.

''McLean!'' Jackson yelled, then broke into a run, cursing under his breath as he raced down the road. Behind him, he heard Hunter answer his shout. He didn't wait.

When he reached the railing around the training arena at the Ericson ranch, he glanced around for a lariat.

Inside the fence, Dawn held on as the horse she rode bucked and twirled in a tight circle. The gelding reared, then straightened, shot all four legs into the air and landed in a flat-out run.

He saw the horse was going to take the fence. He jumped to the second rail, shouting and waving his arms. The gelding veered to the side and circled again, throwing his rear legs high into the air as he dashed around the paddock.

"Get off him!" Hunter yelled, appearing beside him on the fence.

"Can't!" Dawn clung grimly to the saddle, her body moving in rhythm with the animal.

"I'll get a rope," Jackson said. He ran into the stable, grabbed a lasso and entered the paddock.

The gelding came to a standstill, his head down, his sides heaving when he saw Jackson. Dawn talked quietly to the horse, then slid from the saddle. Her legs were trembling.

Jackson scooped her into his arms and carried her to the fence where Hunter waited. "Get out of here," he ordered. He turned back to the gelding, murder in his eyes.

"Check his saddle blanket. He was okay until I put my weight on him," Dawn advised. She straddled the top rail and mopped her face on her sleeve.

Jackson calmed himself and spoke to the horse in soothing tones. The gelding didn't move, except for the nervous twitch in the sweating hide, as he removed the saddle and blanket. He brought both over to the others. They examined the blanket.

"Here's the problem," he said, finding a long spiky thorn embedded in the fabric at an angle.

"Yeah," Hunter agreed. "When Dawn sat down, it pushed the thorn through the blanket and into his hide."

"I'll check his side and rub some antibiotic salve on," Jackson volunteered. He led the horse into the stable and tended him.

He heard Dawn exclaim as she examined the thorn, "How did I pick that up, I wonder?"

"You've been out on the trail a lot the past few days," Hunter reminded her.

Jackson returned from the stable. "Maybe someone planted the thorn." His gaze was hard with suspicion.

"It could have worked its way under the saddle by itself." Hunter examined the spot where Jackson had removed the thorn. "It was slanted in the right direction for that to occur. It's happened to me a time or two."

Dawn nodded. "I'll have to be more careful. The gelding has been saddle-bred from birth. He may never recover from the shock."

"Give him a bucket of oats and a few days for the wound to heal, and he'll forget," Jackson advised.

Dawn climbed down and rubbed her backside. "Or he'll make a fine rodeo bucker."

Jackson found himself chuckling with McLean at her injured expression.

"You're one hell of a rider," Hunter commented. "You thinking about joining the rodeo circuit?"

"No way. I won't be able to sit for a week after the pounding I took."

"Liniment will help," Jackson said, then immediately pictured rubbing it into her backside. He nearly burst his zipper at the thought.

A blush lit up Dawn's face. Jackson smiled with grim satisfaction, knowing she had correctly read his thoughts and was having a few of her own. He glanced at McLean and found the eyes that eerily matched his own studying him with a warning in their depths.

Jackson wondered if he was being told to stay away

from Dawn. He shifted his stance. McLean, with his gimpy leg, wasn't in shape to do battle, but it was best to be prepared in case he tried.

"Good idea," Dawn finally said. She walked toward her house. "I'll use it after my shower." She left the two men standing there.

McLean started up the road. Jackson fell into step beside him.

"What are you going to do about her?" McLean asked.

"Nothing."

"Then she's fair game?"

His whole body clenched at the callous way McLean put it, but he couldn't deny the insinuation. "She's free to do whatever the hell she wants." He stalked off.

"Good," McLean called after him.

Jackson worked with the horses for the rest of the day, but they were nervy and he was impatient with them. It was an exercise in futility. At midafternoon he gave up. After cleaning up, he decided to head for town. He needed to get away from the ranch before he went out of his mind.

In fact, he couldn't figure out why he was hanging around. McLean had been out of action and the fall work had needed doing. That was mostly done. Why was he still here?

He jumped into the truck and took off. A quarter mile down the dusty road he tromped the brakes and came to a halt at the Ericson house.

Dawn was sitting on a pillow under the shade of an oak. J.J. and the pup played hide-and-seek around her and the tree. It was a scene right out of a Norman Rockwell illustration—homey, peaceful, inviting....

Longing to go to her rose in him, drowning out reason and caution. He reminded himself he was the outsider, always would be. Dawn and Hunter belonged here, on this land. They would have a life together.

When he was gone. When she got over the mad passion they shared and she realized where her feelings really lay. Then she would forget him and get on with her real life.

The pain hit him, coming out of nowhere, plunging straight into his heart. He could hardly breathe....

"Would you like to grill some steaks for supper?" she called. "Mom and Margaret are going to a social at church. Hunter is taking J.J. to a birthday party at the home of a friend. We're on our own."

He fought the need to say yes. If he stayed, he knew where they would end up. Briefly he wondered what her bedroom looked like. He stifled the thought.

"I have a date," he said. The statement came out bald and crude and mean. He thought it even sounded truthful.

Her eyes widened in shock. She'd obviously never thought of him with another woman. She blinked once, then again. "Have a nice evening," she said. "Come on, J.J. It's time to go home."

She rose and lifted the child into her arms. As a shield between them, the kid was effective. He stood for all the reasons she belonged with the legitimate McLean brother and not with him. The pup danced around her feet as she walked up the road.

Jackson noted her stride wasn't loose-limbed and flowing. She was already stiffening up from her wild ride that afternoon. He thought of liniment and rubbing it into her tender flesh. He pictured other things they could do after he'd rubbed her down.

Feeling like the bastard he was, he stepped on the gas, determined to go to town and forget the woman with hair like silver and eyes like the sky....

"Dance, honey?"

Jackson glanced up from his beer. A bleached blonde stood beside the table. She gave him an engaging smile. Her makeup looked as if it had been laid on with a trowel. His inclination was to refuse, then he reconsidered.

"Yeah," he said, standing. "I'm here to have a good time. So far it's been a bust."

They went to the dance floor where couples writhed and jumped about in what passed for dancing. He was hit with a case of homesickness that felt close to terminal.

"When I was a kid, my grandfather and I used to dance," he said. "It was a long time ago." His voice sounded thick with sorrow.

The blonde seemed to think that was hilarious. "Your grandpa taught you how to dance? Fun-ny." She broke the word into two equal syllables.

He didn't see anything humorous about it. "Tribal dances."

"You Indian? Excuse me, Native American." She grinned and winked at him. "I wouldn't have thought it. Those green eyes threw me off."

"My father wasn't. He was John McLean."

"Huh," she said.

He remembered he'd driven all the way to Reno to escape. People here didn't bow to the McLean name like they did at the ranch. He smiled at the cynical thought, then frowned as the image of the woman he had left behind appeared in his inner vision.

She seemed to watch him without smiling. He couldn't read the expression in her eyes.

"What are you doing?"

He blinked at the question. He realized he was peering into the hazel eyes of his dance partner as if searching for gold.

"Uh, nothing. You have pretty eyes."

"Oh, why, thanks. They're mostly green, but not many people notice. Everyone thinks I have brown eyes."

"Brown eyes are pretty," he assured her. "And green ones." He thought he should cover all bases.

The dance ended.

"You want to buy me a drink, honey? A man shouldn't drink alone."

In spite of her hair and makeup, he realized she looked as lonely as he felt. It was a hard world for those who didn't belong somewhere or to someone.

"Sure."

After he ordered for her, he nursed his beer and listened to the cadence of her harmless chatter without actually hearing the words.

He checked his watch. Midnight. Still about six hours until dawn. At that word, pale blue eyes peered at him as if through a mist. He tried to peer into them, but they receded and disappeared.

His insides clenched into a hard knot of need. He wondered how long it took to get over a woman. Maggie. She would know. He stood and dropped some bills on the table.

"You leaving, sugar?" The woman looked disappointed.

"Sorry, I have a...an appointment." He tried to recall if she'd told him her name, but couldn't. He shook hands solemnly and left her.

The cold night air snapped him out of the strange haze that had followed him since he'd left Dawn at her place. He drove to his aunt's house. A light was on.

Maggie opened the door before he knocked. "So. It's you," she said. "I knew someone was coming."

"Couldn't you see my face in the smoke?" he asked, only half teasing. His aunt hit the truth too often for him to discount her spirit visions totally.

"I had a feeling it was you. Your cousin saw you at the stock show a while back. You were with a pale-skinned woman. Is she the reason you're here?"

He winced, then stepped inside and let her close the door. "Got any coffee? My mind seems in a muddle."

"You been drinking?" Maggie was a stickler about alcohol.

"One beer. I'd planned to get drunk, but it didn't work. I wanted to show them I could have a good time, but I didn't. That's when I knew I had to come here."

"It's your spirit then." She went into the tiny kitchen and prepared coffee. "I could see your life energy was low when I opened the door. What's wrong? Things not working out over at your father's place?"

"There's someone—" He stopped, not sure he wanted to share Dawn with his acerbic-tongued aunt.

"A woman," she concluded.

"Dawn. Her name is Dawn."

"Are you in love with her?"

"There's this...pull between us. But there's McLean, my half brother. She grew up with him. And his kid. She's the boy's aunt and she's helped raise him. They belong there. I don't."

Maggie studied him for several seconds. "It's the sickness of the heart," she said softly, sorrowfully. She poured the coffee and sat on the sofa beside him. "Tell me about her."

"We met in the woods. She and her mother raise herbs. She's sort of a medicine woman and she's good with horses."

"That makes it harder."

He didn't ask how his aunt knew that each tiny perfect thing about Dawn increased the distance between them, making it harder to leave her while making it impossible to stay.

"She cares about people," he explained. "She respects them and their ways. She didn't laugh when she heard my song in the woods. I had caught a rabbit and was thanking its spirit for giving me sustenance."

"She sounds like a woman of rare understanding."

"Sometimes she is." His face hardened as he frowned. "At others, she's just plain stubborn."

"Ah," Maggie said and nodded.

"That day in the woods, the day we met, she knew who I was. She shared her food with me, knowing I was her enemy."

"And she wasn't afraid of you?"

He shook his head. "Never. She said she wouldn't let me use her to get back at McLean. But there was an attraction. I thought I would win her and laugh at McLean and his loss, but now I see it was a childish thing to do. It was a boy's revenge, and now I'm caught in it."

Maggie clasped one of his hands in hers. "Is she in love with you?"

"She thinks she is. We have this…incredible passion. I tried to explain to her that it doesn't mean anything. I remember how it was between my mother and father. It didn't last. Only family ties, the bond of blood, bind forever. She doesn't listen to me."

He sighed. There, he'd said it all. His spirit didn't feel any lighter, but maybe his aunt could tell him how to get over this longing. It was making him sick, the same way it had when he'd been a boy and his father had stopped coming to see them. It had made him ache clear to his soul.

His aunt opened his fist and studied his palm. "This line—the heart line—is long and unbroken. You will love but one woman, and you will love her always."

He pulled away. "Palm reading isn't Native American."

"Sometimes other cultures have truth."

He grimaced. "The truth is she belongs with Mc-Lean."

"Ask yourself if this woman is the one."

"She would have married him if I hadn't appeared."

"She must choose her own path." Maggie blew across her coffee cup, then sipped carefully.

He took a gulp of the strong brew. The heat and caffeine cleared his head somewhat. His confusion grew not from alcohol but from the conflict within him—the longing to have that which he couldn't.

"I once saw a figurine in a museum. It was the most beautiful and delicate thing I had ever seen. She's like that."

"Perhaps her heart is strong."

"I'm not good for her. She would lose those she loves."

"You must let her choose."

He made an impatient sound. "Both of you are listening women, but neither of you will hear the truth."

Maggie nodded. "You have tried telling her this truth, I take it?"

"More than once. She said our truths might not be the same ones and I had to find my own." He sighed. "Her talk is as roundabout as the old medicine man's who used to visit Grandfather when I was a kid. He talked in circles."

"'The road of life goes but one way,'" she quoted an old proverb her father—his grandfather—had often used. "But perhaps the way is a circle." She stood. "Do you want me to make up the spare bed for you?"

He stared into the coffee cup. "No. I'll return to the ranch. For now. I'll tell her I'm leaving."

"Good. You are not a coward. But be careful that fear isn't whispering lies to your heart and leading you astray. Coyote laughs when he tricks us."

"There," he muttered. "You're doing it, too. Talking in circles," he said to her inquiring look.

She smiled and patted his shoulder. "Here, take the coffee with you. You have a good hour's drive to get home."

He left for the ranch, not sure if he felt any better for having talked to Maggie or not. At any rate, he was more confused about Dawn.

Watching her with Hunter and J.J., he'd decided he had to give her up. He couldn't rip her from the bosom of her family and make her an outcast like himself.

He wouldn't be selfish the way his father had been in taking his mother's love and giving her damn little in return—other than heartache. He wouldn't do that to a woman—any woman—but especially not to Dawn.

By the time he arrived at the ranch, he had looked at the situation from every angle and knew he was right. He had to be the wise one since Dawn wouldn't see reason. Aunt Maggie was a woman and as misty-eyed as any other when it came to male-female relationships. And that was the truth.

Having reached a logical conclusion, he jumped on the porch and nearly tripped over a bundle in the shadows. When he opened the door, the tabby walked inside with a soft meow, as if to remind him she'd been waiting for hours.

"I'm going to be leaving soon, so why are you hanging out here?" he demanded.

The cat gave him a disdainful stare, settled in her favorite spot and went to sleep.

Chapter Thirteen

Dawn shifted to her side and hiked the covers up over her shoulders. The night air was cold. She could feel it blowing across her face and realized she'd forgotten to close the window.

She opened her eyes and peered at the glowing digits on the clock. Eleven minutes after three.

Hearing an engine on the road, she went on instant alert, knowing it must be Jackson. At least he hadn't spent the night with another woman. Unless he'd brought one home with him.

Anger flared and died. He wouldn't do that. He knew it would hurt her. But maybe he wanted to. Maybe what he'd felt was only passion and not the great undying love she thought they had found.

She sighed. Maybe it was time she grew up and

left fantasy behind. Jackson was right. She and Hunter had shared a lifetime of memories. They belonged...

Tears stung her eyes and nose, shocking her. She wasn't a crying person. Her grief was expressed in long, lonely walks or rides, until she could handle it.

And she certainly wasn't grieving over one stupid male.

Feeling around in the dark, she located the box of tissues and mopped her eyes and blew her nose. Piling another pillow behind her, she sat up and watched the faint play of moonlight on the trees and meadows.

She could see the white mare racing along the paddock fence at the McLean ranch. The animal looked ghostly and ethereal. The stallion, in the next enclosure, whickered. Dawn finally spotted him as an inky shadow against shadows.

The mare and the stallion were restless. She wondered if Jackson had succeeded in breeding them. The thought of their offspring had her teary again.

Against the stable, she could see his pickup, parked in its usual place. She wondered if he would clear a path through the trees and build a garage onto his house. In the winter, it would be a cold walk up the slope....

He wouldn't be there, come winter, he'd said.

She heaved a deep breath, sadness echoing through her like a refrain. It was odd—to feel so sad.

Well, morning came early and she would have chores to do. She glanced at the house on the hill and realized she hadn't seen a light come on to indicate he was home. She looked back at the truck.

With a puzzled frown, she realized she could see

the pickup more clearly now. It seemed to be outlined against a glow from the stable.

"Oh, my God!" she whispered and leaped from the bed.

She turned on the lamp and dialed Hunter's number. "I think there's a fire in the stable," she said when he mumbled sleepily into the phone. "I can see a glow through the cracks."

He cursed and hung up.

She threw on jeans and a T-shirt, socks and boots and headed out, grabbing her jacket at the door. "Mom, fire at the stable," she yelled on her way out.

The keys were in the car as usual. She drove the quarter mile and stopped a safe distance from the stables.

Flames erupted from the roof of the building. Sparks flew upward in a giant fireworks display. Men were spilling out of the bunkhouse, half dressed, hopping while they pulled on boots. Hunter was already linking hoses from a spigot by the hay barn.

She ran to Jackson's pickup. No one inside. He needed to move it before it, too, burned. At the very least, the paint would be blistered. She looked at the dark house and wondered what he was doing. She tried not to think of another woman in there with him.

The wind was blowing the sparks that way. The place could catch on fire. She checked the truck. The door was unlocked. The keys were in the ignition.

The scent of aftershave, road dust and ranch stock filled her nostrils when she climbed in and adjusted the seat forward a bit. She didn't detect any strange perfume.

Ignoring a sense of relief, she cranked the engine and drove the truck down the road to where her car was parked. One of the ranch hands followed behind her in the ranch pickup, another with the tractor and hay wagon.

Hunter had two men moving cattle and horses out of the near paddocks and fields and into the pastures. Russ and Larry sprayed water over the big barn and sheds.

After parking, she raced back to the stable. Anna and Margaret were on the patio in their robes, watching the action across the way. There was still no sign of Jackson.

After a second's hesitation, Dawn decided she'd have to go to the house to check on him. He must have gone to bed and fallen instantly asleep. She ran all the way up the steep slope and, skipping the steps, landed on the porch with a single bound. She beat on the door.

No answer.

She tried the knob. The door opened. The hair stood up on her neck. The house felt...unwelcoming.

Ignoring a sense of trespassing, she flicked on the kitchen light and dashed into the new addition, heading for the bedroom where she'd stayed with him, dreading what she might find.

She found nothing.

The bed hadn't been slept in. He wasn't in any of the unfurnished bedrooms or the bathrooms. She called his name. No answer. He wasn't in the house.

Heart racing, she checked the entire house again.

He wasn't there unless he was playing games with her. She fled outside and stopped on the porch.

The fire nibbled at dried blades of grass along the perimeter of the stable, clawing its way along the planking, hissing when the water hit. One end of the stable burst open with a roar, engulfed in flickering tongues of flame the color of molten lava. Clouds of smoke and steam rose toward the bright opalescent face of the moon.

She shivered. Her jacket was in the car. She'd forgotten it when she parked. Wrapping her arms across her middle, she searched among the figures outlined by the burning building.

Jackson wasn't among them. He wasn't anywhere that she could find. She stared at the flames, thinking.

He'd come home. She knew he had arrived. She'd heard the sound of his pickup on the road, going past her house. The truck was here.

Where was he?

The stable. He had to be in the stable.

The thought exploded in her mind, then reverberated through her body. Fear took a chunk out of her heart.

"Jackson!" she cried and started running—straight for the stable.

"Dawn, keep back!" Hunter yelled at her when she threw up a hand to shield her eyes.

"Hunter, Jackson's in there! He has to be. He isn't at home. He wasn't in his truck. He's inside!" She dashed toward the searing heat.

Hands caught at her shoulders.

"Are you crazy? You can't go in there."

She twisted out of Hunter's hands and ran around the building, looking for a way in. Cold water hit her, blinding her and bringing her to a standstill. She turned her head as Russ sprayed her in the face.

Ducking underneath the spray, she scrambled over the paddock fence and entered the stable from the side door. Smoke scorched her lungs. She cupped her arm over her mouth, filtering the smoke somewhat through her wet sleeve.

Behind her, she heard Hunter call her name. "I've got to find Jackson!" she yelled back.

She heard noise behind her. Hunter entered the same door. He brought a hose with him. The water seemed to clear a path through the smoke. She could see inside the burning building now.

Hunter propped the door open and pulled the hose farther inside. The night breeze brought fresh air in through the open door. The fire bellowed outward at the other end.

"The tack room!" she called. "That's where the fire is. I'll check the stalls."

None of the horses were inside, she noted. Jackson usually brought the mare in at night because she could open the gate, but not the stall door.

"Jackson," she yelled. "Jackson, answer me if you're in here. Right now!"

The steady crackling of the fire continued. Fear spread into a black pit of despair inside her. If he was dead...

"We'll find him," Hunter said, keeping a steady spray of water in front of them. He tossed her a wet bandanna. "Use this. The wind is driving the fire out of the building and away from us. That's good."

She swallowed her fear and inched forward, checking every stall thoroughly before moving on. Her lungs burned as if they were on fire as the smoke swirled around them with every shift of the capricious wind.

"He's in the tack room." She caught hold of Hunter's arm. "That's where the fire started."

"If he's in there..." He didn't need to finish the statement. No one could have survived the flames at that end of the building.

She forced herself to search diligently as they moved forward, Hunter cutting a path through the smoke and lashing flames with the water. She squinted against the heat and tried to identify every shape and outline between her and the fire, which seemed less devouring now that the wind was driving it away from fresh fuel.

"There!" she cried, spying a form on the packed-earth floor near the tack-room door. "No... Yes...I think that's—"

Breaking from Hunter, she ran forward. Kneeling beside the inert body, she beat out sparks with her hands. Hunter directed the hose toward them, catching them in a broad arc of lifesaving water.

"Let's get him out of here. Take the hose." Hunter thrust the hose into her hands and caught Jackson under the shoulders. Backing up, with her fighting the fire and Hunter dragging the unconscious man, they made their way toward the safe end of the long building. "Forever" became encapsulated between the fire and the door.

The creak of timber warned that the building might collapse. They made it to the side door and into the paddock. Other hands were there to lift Jackson and carry him to safety up at the main house. Hunter hooked an arm around her waist and helped her in that direction.

Dawn handed the hose to Russ. He stood at the door and used it to wet down the stalls. She broke from Hunter and ran to the patio. Anna was bent over Jackson, her fingers at his wrist, checking his pulse.

"Is he—" Dawn couldn't ask.

"I'm...alive," a deep, croaky voice, barely audible, muttered.

She lifted his head into her lap. "Oh, darling. Oh, my love," she murmured over and over. She checked his face, but saw no burns. She wiped him with the damp bandanna. "I was so afraid. I thought I'd lost you."

"Hell, no such luck," Hunter said, dropping to the patio beside her and coughing up a lungful of smoke. "Anybody that hard to kill will outlive us all."

"Sorry to disappoint you."

Dawn watched the brothers exchange sardonic grins. She frowned, annoyed by their mocking humor. Another McLean trait, she recalled, along with hardheadedness and arrogance.

"Are you hurt?" This came from Margaret, who had watched the little drama on the patio without speaking.

"No, ma'am. Not much," he added at Dawn's protest.

He held still while she inspected him. "Your boots saved your feet," she finally said. "There are holes burned through your jeans in several places."

"I can feel a couple of them," he admitted.

They fell silent and observed the action at the stable.

The fire lost the battle against the water and wind and the grim determination of the men. It spluttered and died. One of the cowboys turned the water off. The quiet was sudden and eerie.

Mrs. Ericson came out of the house. "That was one of the rangers. They spotted the fire. I told them it was under control." She was dressed in slacks and a shirt, but she wore house slippers.

"It's out," Hunter said. He coughed some more.

So did Dawn.

"Let me up," Jackson requested. He pushed himself to a sitting position with a visible effort. Scorched holes dotted his shirt from the tail all the way to his neck.

Her eyes narrowed when she saw him rub the back of his head. "What's wrong?" she asked. "Did you hit your head?"

"Not that I remember, but I have a goose egg, so I must have." He sounded puzzled. "I went to the stable because the mare was out. I couldn't figure out how she'd opened the stall, so I went in to check."

Along with the scent of smoke, the odor of liquor clung to Jackson's lean form. Each time he moved, Dawn caught a strong whiff of it coming from him.

She stiffened when Hunter leaned forward and sniffed.

He stifled a curse, then glared at Jackson. "Damn your hide. You've been drinking. Were you smoking in the stable?"

Jackson glanced at Hunter, gave a contemptuous snort, then pushed to his feet. He didn't bother to answer. Hunter stood, too, his hands fisted. Jackson went on the alert the way a wild creature does when it faces danger.

Dawn stepped between the men. "Of course not. Jackson doesn't smoke." She took Jackson's arm and urged him toward his house before a fight broke out. "You need to rest."

"You got that right," he agreed. "Easy, there," he murmured when she wrapped an arm around his waist.

She recalled the burned places. "Sorry."

"Dawn," her mother said worriedly.

"I'll be all right." She kept a tight grip on Jackson while she guided him off the patio and across the lawn.

At his house, he pushed her away. "I can make it from here. I don't need any nursing."

"You need your back treated. I'm not leaving until I check it, so don't argue."

"Yes, ma'am," he said with facetious meekness.

Once in the house, she started the shower, keeping the temperature tepid because of his burns. Then she pushed him into a chair, pulled off his boots, and peeled him out of his clothing.

"Just like a woman," he muttered. "Taking advantage of a man when he's weak."

She smiled at his corny joke, then told him to get in the shower. In a minute, she was out of her boots, jeans and shirt. She opened the shower door and found him with his back to the water, his head in the crook of his arm, which was propped against the wall. He looked utterly weary.

"Let's get you cleaned up," she suggested, reaching for the shampoo. "You have soot from one end to the other."

"So do you," he retorted. "Get out of here. I can take care of myself."

"I know. Sit down." She switched the shower from the nozzle to a flexible hose and used it to wet his hair once he was seated on the built-in marble bench.

Carefully, lovingly, she soaped his hair, then his lean body. She exclaimed at the burn marks, mostly on his back, a few on his thighs.

She hesitated, then washed him intimately, wondering why she should feel constrained when she'd touched him this way when they'd made love. Then, she'd had his permission. Now she sensed his reluctance.

After a quick shampoo and wash to remove the soot from her own hair and skin, she urged him out of the shower. He had a tendency to close his eyes and lean against whatever was handy.

She dried him off, and then herself. In the medicine cabinet, she found an ointment and rubbed it into every burn she could find.

"My head is pounding like a jackhammer," he told her.

"I know, love, but I can't give you anything for it. You probably have a mild concussion."

"Yeah." He rubbed the lump on his head.

"We'll sort it out tomorrow," she promised. She rummaged through his chest of drawers. "Here, put these pajamas on. It'll keep the sheet from rubbing your burns."

He pulled on the bottoms and tossed the top to her. "You need this more than I do."

She shot him a startled glance when he caressed her bare hip. His smile was mocking.

"I'm not dead, honey."

"Thank God," she said soberly. She was in no mood for his cynical teasing. She slipped into the pajama top and buttoned it to the neck. "Get into bed."

For once, he obeyed her without an argument. She went through the house turning off lights and returned. Seeing that he was settled—on his tummy, she noted—she climbed in the other side and turned off the lamp.

"You can't spend the night here."

She sighed, just then realizing how tired she was. "You think you're well enough to throw me out?"

He muttered an imprecation and lay there in stiff disapproval for several minutes. Then, to her surprised delight, he moved over, laid an arm across her and slipped his thigh between hers. His head nestled on the pillow beside hers.

She relaxed and went to sleep.

Chapter Fourteen

Jackson woke to the smell of bacon and coffee the next morning. He lay on the opposite side of the bed from where he usually slept. Dawn's warm scent lingered on the pillow. He inhaled deeply, recalling the feel of her body against his all night. It hadn't been a dream.

But, he thought, there would probably be hell to pay. For both of them.

Everyone on the ranch had seen her come home with him last night. The sun was long up and she was still there, busy in the kitchen. It would be obvious to a dunce that she'd spent the night. He dressed and padded into the kitchen in his socks.

"Hi. How do you feel?" she asked, spotting him standing in the doorway. "Come sit down. Breakfast is almost ready. Would you like a glass of juice?"

"Please." He took his usual chair, too tired to argue with her over appearances.

She poured coffee and orange juice and brought them to him. It was an effort not to pull her into his lap. The need to touch her still gripped him. Each time he'd woken during the night, he'd been holding her.

He let his gaze roam hungrily over her while she flipped a pancake in the skillet. She removed bacon from the microwave oven and laid the slices on paper towels. A frown indented a shallow line between her eyebrows.

Studying her face, he decided she looked tired. Her lips and cheeks were pale.

Her shirt and jeans were fresh. He assumed she'd gone home earlier and changed. For some reason, he felt the need to have been with her, to defend her if her mother had said anything about her being with him last night.

One thing he could say to Hunter or her mother in all honesty—nothing untoward had happened. They had both been too tired after the events of the night.

But he wasn't this morning.

He thought of eating, then taking her back to bed. He wouldn't, but he thought about it. The heaviness of spirit descended on him again. His path led away from here. He wouldn't take her with him—

"Here we go," she said cheerfully, setting plates on the table. She took her chair after refilling their cups. She raised her juice glass. "To your good health."

Her smile was rueful, but composed. He was aware of her gaze on him, checking him over.

"You saved my life," he told her. "If you hadn't looked for me in the stable, no one else would have thought to do so. I don't know how to thank you for that."

"Nada," she said, her smile broadening into a grin as she tossed his word back at him.

He found himself smiling. He tried to cool it. He wanted to thank her, then tell her he was leaving. He rubbed the lump on his head. Someone, or maybe everyone, on the ranch hated him enough to try to kill him. To stay would be to put Dawn's very life into danger.

His heart turned to dust at the thought of her being hurt. He knew when to cut his losses. It was better to leave before things went from bad to worse.

Before he could broach the subject, McLean came up the slope and knocked.

"Come in," Dawn called out.

The other man entered, hung his hat on a peg and took a seat. He'd brought his own mug of coffee. He looked haggard, as if he hadn't slept at all that night.

"Cold out this morning," he commented.

Jackson nodded and put aside the last bite of pancake and bacon, his senses already alert for whatever would come next.

But first, there was something he had to say to Dawn. "Thank you. That was the best meal I've ever eaten."

He struggled with the need to say more, to thank her for not being afraid of him, for offering him friendship and for giving him moments of the greatest bliss and the most profound peace he'd ever known. But words could only express so much. He wouldn't show her his heart. To do so was useless. He held the words inside.

Dawn looked pleased by the compliment. He resisted the impulse to lean over the table and kiss her.

"I've had a talk with the foreman this morning," McLean continued. He glanced at Dawn, then back at him. "Russ has decided to retire. He owns a small spread in Arizona with his brother. He and Anna are going to move down there."

"Oh, Hunter," Dawn said. Tears sprang into her eyes, turning them into twin lakes of misery.

Jackson studied the words carefully. They made no sense to him. Neither did her grief. Hunter squeezed Dawn's hand, then picked up his coffee cup. Jackson had a feeling they knew more than he did. It put him at a disadvantage. He nodded, but said nothing.

McLean yawned and rubbed a hand over his face as if to scrub out the night and its puzzles.

"It's for the best," Dawn said, but she looked even sadder.

Jackson absorbed the news and mulled it over. He rubbed the sore spot behind his ear and wondered what he was missing in the conversation, because he sure as hell hadn't figured it out.

"I guess I'll be leaving, too," he said. "Tomorrow."

Two pairs of eyes drilled him—the green ones with displeasure, which was puzzling, the pale blue ones with pain so stark, it rattled him. Then she blinked and it was gone. He unclenched his fist and tried not to look at her again.

"We're going to be shorthanded here this winter," McLean said. "You have the end of the logging season to handle and next year's schedule to plan. The remuda needs care all year."

Dawn stared into the steam rising from the coffee and said nothing.

Jackson decided to lay it on the line. "You want me to stick around so somebody can get another chance to knock me on the head, pour liquor all over my clothes and set the stable on fire?" He shook his head. "Sorry, but nothing here means as much as my life."

Except one thing—and she's the reason I have to leave.

He pushed the words into his heart and slammed the door. No need to dwell on that.

"No one will hurt you," Dawn said, her expression as fierce and protective as a mother cat's. It jumbled his insides and nearly made him forget his resolve to leave. But someone had to look out for her even if she didn't think she needed any help.

"Not now," Hunter agreed. "Larry's leaving."

"The foreman's kid?" The young cowhand had been a prime suspect—right after McLean.

"Yes." Dawn sniffed, pressed the heels of her hands to her eyes, then gazed at him. "Larry was the one who hit him and set the stable on fire. Right?" She glanced at Hunter.

"Right." McLean yawned again. "The kid came and told me after the fire was out. He didn't mean for you to die. He wanted you blamed for setting the stable on fire. He meant to be the one to spot it. He thought he would be a hero and that you would have to leave in disgrace. You know the stereotype—just another drunk Indian who couldn't be trusted with responsibility."

"So what happened?" Jackson inquired cynically. "Did he decide things would work out better if I was gone for real?"

McLean refilled his mug. "Naw, the fire spread a lot faster than he'd expected. Then Dawn spotted it and raised the alarm before he did. That ended his chance to be a hero. He couldn't say anything without implicating himself."

"Was he going to leave Jackson inside?" Dawn demanded.

"According to his story, he was going to dash in and pull Jackson out when again you beat him to the punch and went inside." Hunter ruffled her hair. "That's the trouble with you modern women. You won't let the guys play the hero anymore."

She pushed his hand away. Jackson spared a moment of pity for the young cowboy if this enraged lioness came across him while she was in her present mood. He almost smiled, but the ache was too great.

"Anyway, I figure with the two of us and the four ranch hands, we'll make it through the winter."

"I have business to tend to," Jackson insisted doggedly, his willpower wavering.

He tried to think of something compelling he had to do. Nothing came to mind. Everything he wanted was right here—the space to train the top line of riding horses he intended to breed from the stallion and the mare, a snug home that was nearly finished, and half of a ranch that did well in the cattle and timber business.

And a woman who gave him dreams beyond his wildest imaginings, one who thought she loved him...

Two pairs of eyes drilled him, the green ones with open disgust, the pale blue ones with an opaque quietness that he couldn't read.

"I've wasted a summer here. I have other things to do." He shrugged to indicate that the ranch was a minor part of his life, that he had places to go and people to see.

"Well, hell, I was counting on you to get the stable fixed before winter set in," McLean groused.

Jackson stubbornly held his ground. "Sorry."

McLean pushed his chair back and stalked to the door. "You're a coward, a lily-livered skunk who quits at the first sign of trouble. My mother was right. A man would be a fool to depend on a no-account half-breed who's loyal to no one and nothing but himself." He gestured toward Dawn. "You'd be wise to forget him."

Dawn sprang to her feet, a flush highlighting her cheeks, bringing back the color to her face. "That's a terrible thing to say, Hunter."

"It's true. You may be in love with him, but I sure as hell am not. I see him for what he is." He grabbed his hat, jammed it on his head and slammed out the door.

Jackson sprang to his feet and went after him. "Just

a damn minute. You can't call me a bunch of names and think you can then walk out.''

Hunter paused with one foot on the porch. ''I'm doing it.'' He let the storm door slam behind him.

By the time he leaped off the planking to the grass, Jackson was hot on his heels. He grabbed a handful of shirt and spun the other man around. ''You're going to eat those words, you son of a—*whuff*—''

Hunter plowed into Jackson's midsection before the last word got out. Dawn pressed a hand between her breasts and stared in horror as they rolled down the grassy slope to a level spot beside the paddock. She raced after them.

Hunter landed facedown on the bottom of the human mound. Jackson twisted the other man's arm behind his back and toward his neck. ''You give?'' he asked in a snarl.

''Yeah,'' Hunter said in the same tone.

Dawn breathed a sigh of relief. Across the way, she saw Margaret, the yellow cat and her mother come out on the patio. Seeing the fight, they, too, hurried to the scene.

The two men stood, watching each other warily.

''Jackson,'' Dawn said. She wanted to talk to him alone.

When he flicked a glance her way, Hunter stepped forward. Jackson whipped his gaze back to the other man and dropped into an alert crouch.

''Two out of three,'' Hunter said and plowed into him headfirst, taking them to the ground again.

Dawn saw they were going to wrestle rather than box. She sighed in disgust. ''Men,'' she muttered and walked over to stand beside the two older women until the match played itself out. "Where's J.J.?"

"With Anna at the house," Margaret replied.

Hunter, using his greater brawn, pinned Jackson in the second round. Dawn checked her watch. That had taken almost twenty minutes. "You may as well sit," she suggested to her mother, plopping down on the grass. "This is going to take a while."

The cat lay down beside her and watched the two men with a curious feline expression. After a minute, she yawned and laid her head on Dawn's knee.

After ten minutes, when it was obvious neither man was going to give an inch, Margaret rolled forward. She clapped her hands together smartly. "Enough. I'll call the boys over and separate you two."

As if by mutual consent, the men broke apart and lay on the grass panting, their eyes closed.

"I hope we're not going to be subjected to these brutish exhibitions often," Margaret reprimanded them both in the snooty girl's-boarding-school tone she was so good at when the mood struck her.

"No, ma'am," Jackson said, rubbing his ribs. He stood and started back up the slope.

"She loves you, you idiot." Hunter called to his back. "Are you going to walk away from that?"

Jackson stopped as if rooted to the ground. He spun around and shot Hunter a furious glance. "Stay out of it."

"Yeah, you're right," Hunter jeered as if Jackson had said something entirely different. "She's too good for you, but you're her choice." He pushed himself to his feet. "You hurt her and I'll beat the hell out of you seven ways from Sunday. That's a promise.''

Jackson's face turned a dull red.

''Hunter,'' Dawn protested, her face flaming, too. ''You can't make him stay just because…well, because.''

''You have any feelings for her?'' Hunter demanded, ignoring her embarrassment.

Dawn jumped to her feet. ''I'm going to kill *you* if you don't shut up.''

Hunter patted her shoulder. ''It's okay, sweet pea. It's time he figured out what his intentions are. You're not going to sit around waiting for him to make up his mind forever. I'll see to that.''

Jackson took a threatening step forward. ''Damn you—''

''Make up your mind—her or nothing,'' Hunter challenged.

''Really, Hunter,'' Mrs. Ericson scolded. She gave her daughter a pitying glance.

''Hell,'' Jackson muttered. He took two steps and grabbed Dawn's hand. ''Come on. We need to talk.''

''Thirty minutes, then I come after you,'' Hunter warned. He groaned and pressed his knuckles into the small of his back. ''Let's go to the house for a cup of coffee and two aspirin, ladies,'' he invited. He ushered the two mothers up the road. The cat followed at a leisurely pace.

Dawn went along with Jackson as a means of keeping the fragile peace, she told herself, not because she had anything to say to the—the savage.

Inside, he let her go, poured coffee into his mug

and leaned against the counter, his eyes on her as he sipped.

She studied him. "Are you really leaving?"

He cleared his throat. "I was thinking about it."

"Why?"

"I thought there was nothing for me here."

"You've made a home for yourself." She gestured at the house. "You've proved yourself to Hunter and the ranch hands, to everyone in the county. Why would you leave? This was what you came for—to make them recognize and accept you, wasn't it?"

He nodded. That was exactly why he'd come.

"You succeeded. You have everything you wanted, yet you're going to walk away?"

"You don't understand." Hunter didn't, either. Neither of them knew he was worried about her and her happiness. What if she wished she hadn't married him ten years from now? What if she didn't love him then?

"Neither do you." She headed for the door.

An arm curved around her waist and hauled her against a warm, solid chest. He set the cup down. "Don't go," he whispered into her hair.

She folded her arms over his. "Why not?"

"Because."

She leaned into him and rubbed against him, loving the feel of him against her. "The other night, when I asked you to love me, you said, 'I do.' Then you said, 'I will.' Which did you mean?"

It seemed to her that the world held its breath while she waited for his answer. She felt a tremor course down his lean, hard body.

"Both," he murmured, his arm tightening around her.

She twisted around to face him. He looked troubled. "Why aren't you happy about it?"

"I'm the outsider—"

She laid a hand over his lips and shook her head. "Hunter has accepted you. My mother will, too, because she loves me. When she realizes what a good person you are, she'll love you, too. Margaret has come to see you in a different light. She might not learn to love you, but she'll tolerate you."

His chest moved against hers as he snorted in disbelief. "You really think that?"

"I know it. You've made a place for yourself here if you choose to stay and take it. If you leave..." She let the thought trail off.

Jackson gazed into her beautiful eyes. They were as pale and translucent as moonstone, as sincere as a promise, as true as a loyal heart could be. He could feel something inside breaking into pieces, and in its place came a warm, flooding sensation. He knew what it was.

Love. Love flooding his soul, washing away the past and the uncertainties. He saw a future he'd never thought to have, one filled with the good things. The loving things. The passion. The friendship. The sharing.

He lifted her into his arms. "Marry me," he said, suddenly desperate to tie her to him in all ways both legal and holy.

She nodded, her face radiant. "Of course."

The soreness from the fire and from the tussle with

Hunter magically disappeared as he carried her to the bedroom he'd built for her. He placed her on the bed as if she would shatter at the lightest touch.

Sitting beside her, he kissed her for a long time. As their kisses deepened, he felt the bed lift and hover. He smiled, letting his imagination take over.

They floated out the window. He saw McLean on the patio with his son, a toy train going around its track in an endless circle. Like time, he thought, the cycle of the seasons, year in and year out, the same but ever changing.

When they reached the magic glen, he lay beside his mate and slowly stripped them of their clothing. He took his time, savoring each touch, each act of love.

"How soon can we be married?" he asked.

"Today. In Reno," she replied.

"No, in church so everyone can see you chose me." He smiled, so incredibly happy it moved him just to look at her. "Two weeks from now?" he asked.

"Yes." She trailed her fingers over his chest. "The anger is gone," she murmured. "I've felt it around you since you arrived. It's gone."

"I don't need it now." He saw she understood that it had been a shield between him and the world. But then, she had understood everything from the first.

"I'm glad." She snuggled against him.

"Let's have a child right away," he said. "As soon as possible." He wanted to share that with her. They would finish their home and furnish it with children and love.

"Yes," she whispered, touching him intimately, gathering him close, bringing him into her, making them one.

"Dawn," he said, needing the sound of her name on his lips. She didn't know—she might never know—all that she was to him. But he knew.

Dawn. The beginning of light...

* * * * *

Now it's time for the other ornery McLean to find the right woman. See Hunter get roped into marriage in FATHER-TO-BE, SE #1201, this October's THAT'S MY BABY! title.

Silhouette

SPECIAL EDITION

That's My Baby!

Don't miss these heartwarming stories coming to
THAT'S MY BABY!—only from
Silhouette Special Edition®!

**June 1998   LITTLE DARLIN'
by Cheryl Reavis (SE# 1177)**

When cynical Sergeant Matt Beltran found an abandoned
baby girl that he might have fathered, he turned to compassionate foster mother Corey Madsen. Could the healing
touch of a tender family soothe his soul?

**August 1998   THE SURPRISE BABY
by Nikki Benjamin (SE# 1189)**

Aloof CEO Maxwell Hamilton married a smitten Jane Elliott
for the sake of convenience, but an impulsive night of
wedded bliss brought them a surprise bundle of joy—and a
new lease on love!

**October 1998 FATHER-TO-BE
by Laurie Paige (SE# 1201)**

Hunter McLean couldn't exactly recall fathering a glowing
Celia Campbell's unborn baby, but he insisted they marry
anyway. Would the impending arrival of their newborn
inspire this daddy-to-be to open his heart?

**THAT'S MY BABY!
Sometimes bringing up baby can bring surprises...
and showers of love.**

Available at your favorite retail outlet.

Take 2 bestselling love stories FREE

Plus get a FREE surprise gift!

Special Limited-Time Offer

Mail to Silhouette Reader Service™

> 3010 Walden Avenue
> P.O. Box 1867
> Buffalo, N.Y. 14240-1867

YES! Please send me 2 free Silhouette Special Edition® novels and my free surprise gift. Then send me 6 brand-new novels every month, which I will receive months before they appear in bookstores. Bill me at the low price of $3.57 each plus 25¢ delivery and applicable sales tax, if any.* That's the complete price, and a saving of over 10% off the cover prices—quite a bargain! I understand that accepting the books and gift places me under no obligation ever to buy any books. I can always return a shipment and cancel at any time. Even if I never buy another book from Silhouette, the 2 free books and the surprise gift are mine to keep forever.

235 SEN CH7W

Name	(PLEASE PRINT)	
Address	Apt. No.	
City	State	Zip

This offer is limited to one order per household and not valid to present Silhouette Special Edition® subscribers. *Terms and prices are subject to change without notice. Sales tax applicable in N.Y.

USPED-98

©1990 Harlequin Enterprises Limited

International bestselling author

JOAN JOHNSTON

**continues her wildly popular Hawk's Way
miniseries with an all-new, longer-length novel**

THE SUBSTITUTE GROOM

HAWK'S WAY

August 1998

Jennifer Wright's hopes and dreams had rested on her summer wedding—until a single moment changed everything. Including the *groom*. Suddenly Jennifer agreed to marry her fiancé's best friend, a darkly handsome Texan she needed—and desperately wanted—almost against her will. But U.S. Air Force Major Colt Whitelaw had sacrificed too much to settle for a marriage of convenience, and that made hiding her passion all the more difficult. And hiding her biggest secret downright impossible...

**"Joan Johnston does contemporary Westerns
to perfection."** *—Publishers Weekly*

Available in August 1998
wherever Silhouette books are sold.

Silhouette®SPECIAL EDITION®

Newfound sisters Bliss, Tiffany and Katie
learn more about family and true love
than they *ever* expected.

A new miniseries by
LISA JACKSON

A FAMILY KIND OF GUY (SE#1191) August 1998
Bliss Cawthorne wanted nothing to do with ex-flame
Mason Lafferty, the cowboy who had destroyed her
dreams of being his bride. Could Bliss withstand his irresistible charm—the second time around?

A FAMILY KIND OF GAL (SE#1207) November 1998
How could widowed single mother Tiffany Santini be
attracted to her sexy brother-in-law, J.D.? Especially
since J.D. was hiding something that could destroy the
love she had just found in his arms....

And watch for the conclusion of this series in
early 1999 with Katie Kinkaid's story in
A FAMILY KIND OF WEDDING.

Available at your favorite retail outlet. Only from

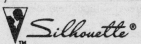

COMING NEXT MONTH

#1195 EVERY COWGIRL'S DREAM—Arlene James
That Special Woman!
Feisty cowgirl Kara Detmeyer could handle just about anything—except the hard-edged stockman escorting her through a dangerous cattle drive. Rye Wagner had stubbornly insisted he'd never settle down again, but a daring Kara had *every* intention of roping in the man of her dreams!

#1196 A HERO FOR SOPHIE JONES—Christine Rimmer
The Jones Gang
Vowing to reclaim his father's lost land, ruthless Sinclair Riker embarked on the heartless seduction of beguiling Sophie B. Jones. But Sophie's sweet, intoxicating kisses had cast a magical spell over him—and he ached to do right by her. Could love transform Sin into Sophie's saint?

#1197 THE MAIL-ORDER MIX-UP—Pamela Toth
Winchester Brides
Travis Winchester fought an irresistible attraction to his missing brother's mail-order bride. Even though he didn't trust Rory Mancini one bit, he married the jilted city gal after taking her under his wing—and into his bed. But he couldn't stop wonderin' if Rory truly loved her *unintended* groom....

#1198 THE COWBOY TAKES A WIFE—Lois Faye Dyer
Sassy CeCe Hawkins was forever bound to her late husband's half brother, Zach Colby. Not only was her unborn baby heir to the Montana ranch Zach desperately coveted—and half-owned—but a forbidden passion for this lonesome, tight-lipped cowboy left her longing for a lifetime of lovin' in his arms.

#1199 STRANDED ON THE RANCH—Pat Warren
When sheltered Kari Sinclair fled her overprotective father, she found herself snowbound with oh-so-sexy rancher Dillon Tracy. Playing house together would be a cinch, right? Wrong! For Kari's fantasies of happily-ever-after could go up in flames if Dillon learned her true identity!

#1200 OLDER, WISER...PREGNANT—Marilyn Pappano
Once upon a time, tempting teenager Laurel Cameron had brought Beau Walker to his knees. Then, she'd lit out of town and left Beau one angry—and bitter—man. Now she was back—pregnant, alone, yearning for a second chance together. Could Beau forgive the past...and learn to love another man's child?